HOMETOWN HEARTS

SHIPMENT 1

Stranger in Town by Brenda Novak
Baby's First Homecoming by Cathy McDavid
Her Surprise Hero by Abby Gaines
A Mother's Homecoming by Tanya Michaels
A Firefighter in the Family by Trish Milburn
Tempted by a Texan by Mindy Neff

SHIPMENT 2

It Takes a Family by W
The Sheriff of Heartbreak C_____ _____ton
A Hometo____
The Renegade____
Unexp____
Accidental _____ ___dge

SHIPMENT 3

An Unlikely Mommy by Tanya Michaels
Single Dad Sheriff by Lisa Childs
In Protective Custody by Beth Cornelison
Cowboy to the Rescue by Trish Milburn
The Ranch She Left Behind by Kathleen O'Brien
Most Wanted Woman by Maggie Price
A Weaver Wedding by Allison Leigh

SHIPMENT 4

A Better Man by Emilie Rose
Daddy Protector by Jacqueline Diamond
The Road to Bayou Bridge by Liz Talley
Fully Engaged by Catherine Mann
The Cowboy's Secret Son by Trish Milburn
A Husband's Watch by Karen Templeton

HOMETOWN HEARTS

Bachelor Dad

ROXANN DELANEY

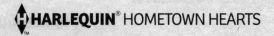

Recycling programs
for this product may
not exist in your area.

ISBN-13: 978-0-373-21493-8

Bachelor Dad

Copyright © 2011 by Roxann Farmer

Printed in U.S.A.

Roxann Delaney doesn't remember a time when she wasn't reading or writing, and she's always loved that touch of romance in both. A native Kansan, she's lived on a farm and in a small town, and has returned to live in the city where she was born. Her four daughters and grandchildren keep her busy when she isn't writing or designing websites. The Maggie Award winner loves to hear from readers. Contact her at roxann@roxanndelaney.com or visit her website, www.roxanndelaney.com.

To the wonderful ladies of WARA (Wichita Area Romance Authors) for their encouragement, support and especially their friendship for the past fifteen years.

Chapter One

Ignoring the lunch crowd at Lou's Place, Garrett Miles skimmed the minutes from Tuesday night's city council meeting and jotted a note on a legal pad. The local tavern might not be the ideal place for the city attorney to be working, but his tiny office in the municipal building had become claustrophobic. Besides, he was hungry.

"Coffee, tea or...?"

Smiling, he looked up and into a pair of familiar amber eyes and a devilish smile. "When did you start working the lunch shift?" he asked.

Libby Carter waited until he'd put his paperwork aside before she placed a cup of coffee in front of him. "Jeanine needed a couple of hours off, so I offered to cover for her. I didn't know you came here for lunch."

A strand of her blond hair had slipped from the twisted knot at the back of her head and fallen along her cheek, and he fought the urge to touch it. He'd always been attracted to Libby and liked her far more than he should.

He pushed the thought aside, smiled again and shrugged. "I had a hankering for one of Kate McPherson's barbecue beef sandwiches and didn't want to wait until after work."

"I can't blame you for that," she answered, tucking the errant strand of hair behind her ear. "Is there anything else I can get you? Besides the sandwich, that is."

Picking up the cup in front of him, he shook his head. "Just the sandwich," he answered. "And keep the coffee coming."

She looked over her shoulder when another customer called to her, and Garrett heard her sigh before she answered. "Be there in a second, Gus." When she turned back to Garrett, she flashed him a smile. "Duty calls. I'll have that sandwich for you right away."

"Thanks."

He watched her walk to the bar where several locals sat, their beer glasses and bottles in hand, their talk quiet except for an occasional burst of laughter. He didn't stop in for lunch at Lou's often, preferring to visit in the evenings after work, but today he'd needed the change of scenery. Seeing Libby was a perk.

Picking up the cup of coffee, he took a drink—and nearly scalded the roof of his mouth, causing him to let out a small yelp.

Libby appeared within seconds with a glass of water. "Too hot?"

He nodded and set his cup down quickly.

She picked it up and sighed. "I told Lou he was serving it too hot. Did he listen? Like he always does, meaning never. I'll get it cooled down." Shaking her head, she hurried to the bar and reached over the top of it.

Garrett stared, instantly forgetting about his burned mouth. He wasn't the only one in the place who was looking. Nearly every man with decent eyesight was watching, the same as he was. It hadn't escaped his notice or anyone else's that Libby's charms included more than being a good waitress with a sassy attitude. She was a very attractive woman. *Especially from the back.*

He'd thought more than once of asking her out, but he'd never done it. He didn't have time, and he wasn't interested in a relationship. Libby might be fun to flirt with at Lou's, but he knew from talking to her that she was a single mom and as far as he was concerned, that was a red light.

"I added some ice," Libby said, hurrying back to his table and setting the cup of cooled coffee in front of him again.

The twinkle in her eyes put him on guard. "What, besides ice, did you put in it?"

"Only ice, I swear," she answered, placing one hand flat on the table and holding up the other. "I want to make sure it's all right. After all, we can't have one of our best customers, not to mention our only non-beer-drinking customer, burning his mouth."

"It's okay," he answered. "I'm good."

"So I've heard."

He couldn't keep from chuckling. Having a conversation with Libby was always a game. "Hassling the injured guy, are you?"

"Get 'em while they're down, I always say." She walked away with an exaggerated swing to her hips. Within minutes, she returned with his sandwich. "On the house," she told him.

"There's no need for that," he assured her, pulling the plate closer. "I'm not going to sue."

He'd expected a smart answer from her, but

instead she said nothing. She looked tired, he thought, noticing the dark circles beneath her eyes, but she always had a smile for everyone.

She leaned forward to wipe a few water rings from the table with the corner of the dishtowel tucked into the waistband of her jeans. "Why hasn't such a nice guy like you settled down with an equally good woman?"

He considered giving her a flippant answer, but instead he decided she deserved honesty. "I practiced family law back in Chicago for several years. You know, divorce and child custody and all that. I thought I could make a difference. Came to find out, I couldn't. No matter how hard I tried, I couldn't keep those kids from being pawns of their parents. Divorce is always messy, even when everybody starts out agreeing, but when kids are involved… Well, I guess you could say the whole experience jaded me."

"I can understand how that could happen," she answered, without looking directly at him.

"What about you?" he asked. "You're divorced, right?"

She nodded as she continued to wipe at a spot on the table, but she didn't say anything.

"What about Noah's dad?" he continued, curious. When she straightened, a frown marring her usually sunny expression, he knew he'd stepped over the bounds. "I'm sorry, it's none of my business."

"No, it's all right. I started it," she admitted with a small smile. "Noah's dad isn't in the picture."

He nodded, accepting her brief answer. Before he could say anything else, his cell phone rang. Pulling it from the pocket inside his jacket, he answered. "Garrett here."

"Garrett, were you expecting a delivery?"

He recognized the voice of Tootie Fredericks, the city administrator. "No. Why?"

"You need to get back to the office, right now."

She sounded upset, and he knew that wasn't a good sign. "What is it, Tootie?"

"A package came for you."

"A package? Can't it wait?"

"No, it can't, and you need to get your butt here right now."

He was accustomed to her eccentricities, chalking them up to her thirty plus years working for the city, and he chuckled softly. Tootie was a great administrator, but sometimes she got carried away. "Why? Will it explode?"

"No," she answered briskly, "but you might. Get a move on."

"But what—?" There was no reason to finish. He heard the empty silence and knew she'd ended the call. Sighing, he looked at the half-eaten sandwich in front of him and quickly caught Libby's eye. "Can you get me something so I can take my sandwich with me?" he asked when she hurried over. "I'd really appreciate it. I have to get back to the office."

"Of course. It'll only take a second." Libby disappeared, taking the sandwich and plate with her.

He'd just finished gathering his paperwork together and was pulling some money from his wallet, when she reappeared with a paper sack and handed it to him. "I hope everything is all right."

"Oh, I'm sure it is. She probably thinks I've taken a long enough lunch today. You know what they say. A man's work is never done."

"I do believe it's a woman's work that's never done," she corrected him, as he moved away from the table.

"Could be." He realized he was wishing he didn't have to leave and knew he shouldn't feel that way. Pressing the bills into her hand, he said, "That should take care of it, with a little extra for you."

She shook her head, but he ignored it and

left the tavern, turning toward the city building, two blocks away. It was a nice day, and he'd chosen to walk to Lou's and enjoy the outdoors. He didn't hurry, suspecting that Tootie simply thought it was time for him to be back at his desk.

As he reached the Chick-a-Lick Café, Morgan Rule, Desperation's sheriff, stepped out and onto the sidewalk. "I didn't see you inside and thought you might be working at home today," Morgan said, joining him.

Garrett explained that he'd gone to Lou's for a change, and they walked on to city hall together. The small building where they both worked sat on the far corner of what was considered the business part of town. Garrett stopped at the first door, while Morgan continued on to the next. Once inside, Garrett passed through the reception area and continued along a hallway.

As he walked by Tootie's office, she stepped out and grabbed him by the arm, leading him to his office.

"What's going on, Tootie?" he asked, tired of whatever game she was playing. "And where's this package?"

"You'll see," she answered, hanging back as he walked into his office and put the paper bag on his desk. When he looked back at her, standing just outside the doorway, she nodded her head. "Go on."

"I don't see any—" He stopped, then shook his head, thinking he was seeing things.

A small girl sat on a nearby chair, her hands folded in her lap. His first thought was that she looked like his sister, and he couldn't imagine how that could be. He was pretty sure she didn't have a daughter.

So who was this child?

He turned to look at Tootie, still standing in the doorway. "Who—?"

"Shush," she whispered, glancing behind him at the little girl. Crooking her finger at him to follow, she directed him outside the door and then pressed an envelope into his hand. "Maybe this will answer your question."

Garrett glanced at the child again and then tore open the envelope. Unfolding the single piece of paper he found inside, he read handwriting that was eerily familiar to him, and he wasn't eager to remember why. It wasn't long before he knew.

Hoping Tootie wouldn't see that his hands had begun to shake, he folded the paper and returned it to the envelope. He wasn't sure he could speak, so he cleared his throat before he tried. "Who brought this?"

She shook her head. "I didn't see her. Geri was up front, and she brought the girl back to me and asked me when you'd be back. I told her you were out to lunch. She said a woman had walked in and asked for you. When Geri told her you were out, she said something about you expecting the girl, handed her that envelope and hightailed it out the door."

He didn't doubt the girl's mother was in and out before anyone could question her. "Did Geri see the car she came in?"

"She said it was a dark color, and it looked like there was a man behind the wheel, but it peeled away so fast, she couldn't get a tag number. But it wasn't an Oklahoma license." Tootie's eyes narrowed as she watched him. "You weren't expecting her, were you?" When he shook his head and avoided looking at her, her sigh was deafening. "What's going on, Garrett?"

He wasn't sure how to say it. If what was in the short letter was true…

"Her name is Sophie," he answered. "Sophie Miles."

"Sophie *Miles?*" Tootie repeated.

He nodded, and his throat tightened around the words he needed to say. "She's my daughter."

Libby watched as the heavy wooden door of the tavern slowly swung shut behind Garrett and reminded herself that she could never get involved with any man, especially him. If he knew the truth… She gave herself a shake. He didn't know and never would.

The old, scarred door swung open again, but it was Jeanine who breezed inside. Hurrying toward Libby, she smiled. "Thanks for filling in for me," she said. "I'll take over. You can go home and rest up before tonight's shift."

"Sounds wonderful," Libby answered and turned to the table Garrett had vacated. "I'll just finish clearing this table and—" Tucked next to the coffee cup Garrett had used was his cell phone. "Looks like Garrett forgot something."

"Maybe you should take it to him," Jeanine suggested, a twinkle in her eye.

Libby knew what her fellow waitress was thinking and decided her best course of action would be to ignore it. "I suppose I should. It will only take a couple of minutes, and then I can go home and sleep until Noah gets home from school."

"Sounds like a plan," Jeanine said. "I'll finish cleaning up."

Libby hesitated. "You're sure?"

Jeanine gave her a gentle shove. "Of course."

"Okay, thanks." Libby pulled the towel from her waistband as she hurried to the bar and stepped behind it. She hadn't slept especially well the night before. Usually she had no problem, but she'd been restless and dreams that bordered on nightmares had plagued her, waking her with a pounding heart. She was sure there was no reason to be worried, and she tried not to, but something would trigger memories she thought were buried, and that's when the dreams would start.

Grabbing her purse from under the bar, she slipped the cell phone inside, then headed toward the door, giving Jeanine a wave as she stepped outside. The early afternoon sunshine was bright, and she blinked as she crossed the gravel parking lot to her car. The car door groaned when she opened it, but she ignored it and slid inside. For a brief moment, she was afraid the car wasn't going to start, but the engine finally took hold, and within seconds she was on her way down the street to the city building.

Within a few minutes, she'd quickly parked

the car, hurried inside and pulled the phone from her purse. Expecting to give it someone at the front desk, she was surprised to find no one there. With a shrug, she moved on and discovered a hallway that she hoped would lead her to the city offices where she'd find Garrett. A few steps later, she heard him before she saw him.

"Why didn't you call me?" he said, his voice not far away.

"I did, if you remember."

Libby could see Garrett and silver-haired Tootie Fredericks standing just inside a small office she suspected was Garrett's. Not wanting to interrupt or appear to be eavesdropping, she stopped and waited. But not overhearing what was being said was impossible. Although Tootie's voice was low, the volume of Garrett's wasn't.

"You gave me some crazy talk about a package." He raked his hand through his hair, leaving part of it sticking straight up. "It wasn't as if you *even gave me a clue*."

"You need to lower your voice," Tootie said, sounding like a teacher reprimanding a student.

Garrett happened to look up at that moment, and Libby knew the moment he saw her. "Sorry to bother you," she said, quickly approaching them and ready to get this little visit over with, "but no one was up front."

Tootie stepped out of the office and into the hallway. "I thought Geri was watching the front."

"You can't leave!" Garrett said as she started to walk away. There was no question in Libby's mind that something had him in a panic. She didn't recall ever seeing him ruffled by anything.

The frown Tootie shot him immediately softened to what might be recognized as a smile by some, and she patted the hand he now had on her arm. "You'll be fine for a minute or two. I'll find Geri. She's probably upset because I lit into her earlier. I'll be right back. Until then, Libby can keep you both company."

"Both?" Libby repeated as Tootie left them. She turned to Garrett. "I'm sorry. I've obviously picked a bad time."

"It's not that." He cleared his throat but said nothing else.

Attempting to ignore his obvious discomfort, she quickly handed him his cell phone. "I stopped by to give you this. You left it at Lou's."

He took the phone from her and shoved it inside his jacket. "Thanks."

"Is something wrong?" she finally dared to ask.

"No," he said, but followed that with a nod. "Okay, yes, there's something wrong." He glanced over his shoulder, and then quickly added, "Not *wrong,* just…"

Libby heard the tap of footsteps coming closer down the hall and looked back to see Tootie. Good. Now she could leave. Whatever was going on with Garrett, she didn't feel comfortable being a part of it. Talking to him at Lou's was one thing. Being around him outside of where she worked was something completely different.

Before she could make a move to leave, she noticed movement out of the corner of her eye. Looking more closely, she saw a small girl sitting perfectly still on a straight-backed metal chair near a tall filing cabinet. The child held a battered teddy bear in her arms.

"Hi, there," Libby said, smiling at the child, and then turned to Garrett. "Daughter of a client?"

"That's a good question," Tootie said, stepping inside the office. "You should answer her, Garrett."

"Libby came to bring me my phone," he explained, ignoring her suggestion. He headed for a coffeemaker near the filing cabinet and poured himself a cup. "I accidentally left it behind at Lou's."

Tootie chuckled at the information. "Saturday he left it at the post office."

All Libby wanted to do at that point was leave. "Yes, well—"

"Would you like some?" he asked Libby, gesturing toward the coffeemaker.

"No, thank you. I really should be going."

"Tootie? How about you? It seems we're having some sort of get-together here."

But Libby was watching the little girl, who slid down from the chair and walked slowly to Garrett. Holding her teddy bear in one arm with what appeared to be a fierce grip, she tugged on the sleeve of Garrett's jacket with her free hand.

He looked down at her as if he was seeing her for the first time. "Do you want something?" he asked carefully.

She nodded and pointed to his coffee cup.

"Oh, mercy me," Tootie exclaimed. "She's thirsty. Don't you dare give her coffee, Garrett Miles. It'll stunt her growth."

Libby had to clamp her mouth shut on the laugh that threatened. "Is there water somewhere?" she asked. "An extra glass or cup, maybe?"

"I have something even better," Tootie said and turned to the little girl. "Do you like milk?"

The child nodded her head and almost smiled.

"We have some in the refrigerator in back for people who use it in their coffee. Why don't you come with me and we'll get you a glass."

The girl took Tootie's hand when she held it out, and they stepped out into the hall. Garrett let out a loud sigh of what was obviously relief, just as Tootie stuck her head back in the door. "Why don't you show Libby that letter? She's a mother. Maybe she can make some sense of it all."

This time Garrett watched them as they walked away. When they'd disappeared around a corner, he shook his head and leaned his hip against his desk. "This is…" His hand went to his hair again, but stopped midway. He turned to Libby, saying, "I'm sorry you were dragged into this."

Concerned that whatever was going on was not only serious but very private, she didn't know what to say. "Since I don't really know what's going on, there's no reason to be sorry.

And before I do know too much, maybe I should go."

She'd taken a step toward the doorway, when he spoke. "I'd rather you didn't." When she glanced back at him, he pushed away from the desk. "I could use a more unbiased yet knowledgeable person to counsel me."

"Knowledgeable? Me?" She couldn't imagine how she could help him. The only thing she knew about that he didn't was how to disappear, and he might even have a clue about that. Her life prior to her arrival in Desperation eight months ago was a closed—and tightly locked—subject, not to mention something she'd rather forget.

"You're a single parent," he answered. "Most of the parents I know these days are couples, although back in the day, I guess I helped couples become single parents."

He didn't appear especially proud of that last part, and she could understand. She also understood that she had to remain silent when it came to her situation and how she managed to get to where she was now. Not only was secrecy about her escape from Phoenix with her son a necessity, but Garrett being a lawyer was a danger, not only to her but to those who had helped her.

And then she thought about what he'd just said. "What does my being a single parent have to do with you?"

He picked up an envelope from his desk, pulled a folded paper from it and handed it to her. "This might answer your question and explain why I'm acting rather strange."

She studied him for a moment, trying to decide if he was kidding. Unable to tell, she unfolded the letter and began skimming the handwriting. It didn't take long before the skimming stopped and the reading began. From what she could tell, it was what people called a kiss-off letter, but it wasn't Garrett who was getting dumped, it was the little girl. Her name was Sophie Miles, and apparently she was Garrett's daughter.

Glancing up at him, she asked, "Were you aware of this?"

He stuffed both hands in his pockets and shook his head. "Not until Tootie gave me the letter."

Libby looked around to make sure no one was nearby. "Are you sure you're the father?" she asked in a whisper.

"She looks exactly like my sister at that age. Right down to the freckles across her nose."

Libby didn't want to make things worse for

him, but even he should know that a resemblance wouldn't stand up in court. "That's definitely a good sign, but—"

"I intend to have a paternity test done, if that's what you're going to say."

She studied him. "You really didn't have a clue?"

"Absolutely none."

By the set of his mouth, she knew she shouldn't push it. Maybe he hadn't known, but whether he had or not wasn't the question. "I guess I should congratulate you," she finally said, not knowing what else she could do. "It isn't every day a man learns he's the father of a four-year-old. And just so you know, you were lucky to miss the diaper and potty training years."

He gripped the coffee cup tightly in his hands and stared into it. "That doesn't convince me that this is going to be easy."

She smiled. "It isn't."

He looked up with a pitiful smile of his own. "Which is why women have babies, not men."

"You just keep thinking that," she replied, swallowing a chuckle.

Their conversation came to a halt when Tootie returned with the little girl. "She's hungry," Tootie announced.

Libby looked at Garrett. "Is that the other half of your sandwich?" she asked, pointing to the sack on his desk. "You could give it to Sophie."

"I don't know why not. I seem to have misplaced my appetite."

Tootie took the sack from Libby and bent down to Sophie. "The break room would be a much better place to have lunch than here in this busy office. Let's take it in there, and I'll get you another glass of milk. How would that be?"

The child nodded, but didn't speak, and as Sophie followed Tootie out the door, Libby wondered why. But before giving any more thought to it, she realized how long she'd been there and that she still had the letter Garrett had given her in her hand. "I'd probably better be on my way," she told him, giving the folded paper back to him. Turning for the door, she was almost in the hallway when she heard him speak.

"She hasn't said anything. Not a single word."

Libby looked back, but wasn't sure how to answer. "She may be shy," she tried, hoping that would ease the lines that had deepened between his gray eyes. "After all, everything here is new to her."

He nodded, but the worry on his face remained. "Including me."

She pressed her lips together, wondering if there was anything she could say that would cushion his shock at learning he was a father. But she didn't feel she knew him well enough to give him advice. "You'll both do fine," she offered, hoping that would help at least a little.

He shook his head. "I don't see how we can. I don't know the first thing about raising a child."

"Neither do most mothers with their first," she pointed out. "But they learn."

"No, women are endowed with maternal instincts."

"Endowed?" she asked, laughing.

"You know what I mean. And I'm serious. I really don't know what to do."

"You'll learn, Garrett, and before you know it, you'll be a great father." At least she hoped he would be. All he really needed was to get off to a good start. To do that he needed— "Why don't you have your sister take a look at Sophie? Make sure she's in good physical shape, and then go from there."

His worry lines eased a little, and a hopeful smile appeared. "You're right. I'll take her to see Paige today. Thanks, Libby."

"You would have thought of it yourself." Before he could deny it, she hurried on. "I'd better be getting home. I'm working the night shift, too, and Noah will be home from school soon."

He nodded. "Thanks again."

"Any time." But something kept her from taking that step away. Surely she could do something else for him. She wouldn't have to get involved, just offer a little support.

"Garrett?"

When his gaze met hers, she saw that his usually bright eyes were clouded with worry. "If you need some help—you know, a question about food or clothes or whatever—let me know."

His eyes cleared, and then his smile slowly appeared, spreading wide. "Yeah. Yeah, I'll do that."

Good grief! she thought as she hurried down the hallway toward the main door. Was she out of her mind? The less she was around Garrett Miles, the better. But, fool that she was, she'd just offered to help.

Chapter Two

Garrett had hoped the waiting room of the small medical clinic where his sister was the only physician would be empty. He should've known it wouldn't be, but hope seemed to be the only thing he had left. He was worried. Sophie hadn't spoken a word since Tootie had taken charge of her at the city building nearly four hours earlier. Even now, as she and Garrett stepped inside the waiting room of the clinic, she was silent, holding his hand with a grip a wrestler would admire while she clung to her teddy bear with her other hand.

Don Fulcom, the husband of one of the nurses, sat in a chair, thumbing through a magazine. He looked up as Garrett and Sophie crossed the room. Garrett nodded in greeting and guessed the man was probably there to pick up his wife.

"Hello, Garrett," Cara Milton said from the other side of the receptionist's window.

Garrett noticed she was trying hard not to stare at Sophie, and he tried just as hard to ignore her obvious curiosity. "Is my sister free?"

She turned to look into the hallway behind her before answering. "Not quite yet, I'm afraid, but she shouldn't be too much longer." She crooked a finger at him, and he leaned closer, hoping she wasn't going to ask him about Sophie. Instead, she asked, "Would you like to wait in her office?"

He looked down at Sophie, so small and silent next to him, and he nodded.

Cara smiled as he crossed to the door that led from the waiting room into the hallway and on to his sister's office. He knew full well that he and Sophie would soon be the talk of the town, especially when, before he was completely out of earshot, he heard a whisper.

"I wonder who that little girl is?" Cara was saying to Don Fulcom.

Garrett didn't wait to hear the answer and doubted Don even had one. With a sigh and a shake of his head, he took Sophie into Paige's office.

"Do you want to sit down?" He pointed to two chairs facing a worn desk that was stacked with medical files and journals.

Sophie hesitated, before climbing onto the chair closest to the wall.

Knowing that news spread fast in Desperation, Garrett wanted to be the one to tell his sister he was a father. Not that he had any idea of how to do it. She'd probably ask questions, and he knew so little, except that Sophie was the result of a relationship with a young woman he'd once thought he might be in love with. It had taken a few months for him to know the real Shana, and once it became clear that she wasn't the kind of person he'd thought she was, he broke it off. A month and a half later, he moved to Cincinnati, where he lived with his sister until he was hired by the City of Desperation.

Nervous, he leaned a hip against the edge of the desk, crossed his arms, smiled at Sophie and waited. He'd learned quickly that trying to have a conversation with a four-year-old who didn't speak—for whatever reason—was pretty much futile. Hopefully Paige could give him a clue as to what was going on, and then he would do whatever was needed to correct the problem. It was that simple.

Several silent minutes later, he heard Paige's voice outside the small office. As the door opened, he pushed away from the desk and gave Sophie what he hoped was an encouraging smile.

"Cara told me you needed to see me?" Paige made it a question as she stepped into the room. For a brief moment, she looked only at Garrett, but when Sophie shifted in the chair, Paige looked down. "Well, hello there!" she greeted Sophie. "I didn't see you." Kneeling to Sophie's level, Paige smiled and stuck out her hand. "My name is Paige. What's yours?"

When Sophie didn't answer, but placed her hand in Paige's, Paige looked up at Garrett, who managed to swallow his nervousness enough to speak. "Her name is Sophie," he answered.

The confusion in Paige's eyes didn't make him feel any calmer, nor did her next question for Sophie. "And who do you belong to?"

His nerves were like pins sticking him when Sophie slowly looked up at him. He had no choice but to answer. After all, that's why he was there to see his sister. "She belongs to me."

Paige slowly turned her head to stare at him, her surprise bordering on disbelief.

"She's my daughter."

Paige's mouth opened, as if she was going to say something, but instead, she closed it and turned back to smile at Sophie. "And how old are you, Sophie?" she asked.

To Garrett's surprise, Sophie held up four fingers.

Standing, Paige turned to him and spoke softly. "I've always wanted a pretty little niece." More quietly, she added, "Is there anything I can do to help?"

Relief washed over Garrett, and he leaned against the desk again. The activities of the afternoon had definitely tested him. At the moment, he wasn't sure he was passing.

"Are you all right?" Paige asked.

He nodded and stood straight. "I'm good." After glancing at Sophie, he turned back to his sister. "I'd feel better if I knew Sophie is okay."

Paige smiled at his daughter. "We can do that." When she opened the door to step outside, Fran Simpson, the other nurse, was in the hallway. "Which examining room can we use?" Paige asked her.

"They're all free. The last of the patients are gone."

"Good," Paige replied. "I'll lock up. You

and Cara and Susan can go on home. I'll see you in the morning."

"Have a good evening," Fran called, her voice coming from farther down the hall.

When Paige motioned for Garrett to follow her, he held out his hand to Sophie, who hesitated at first and then took it. Her tiny hand in his felt fragile as they followed Paige into the hallway, and his heart constricted at the thought of what Sophie's life might have been like before she'd arrived at his office. He didn't have a clue, and now that he thought about it, it scared him. If anything had happened... If anything was wrong with her...

"Right in here," Paige said, stepping into the nearest examining room. She pointed to the padded table. "Put her up there, while I go grab a new chart."

Sophie let go of his hand, and he lifted her onto the table. The paper runner crackled beneath her as she settled on it, and she looked up at him, her eyes wide.

"She's my sister," he said, moving back. "The doctor is," he added. "Do you know what a sister is?"

Sophie shrugged her shoulders.

"So much for that," he muttered.

Paige breezed back into the room, a manila

folder in her hand. "They've all gone, so there won't be any interruptions. Is there anything special I'm looking for?"

"Anything," he answered. "Everything. I just want to know that she's okay. Healthy."

Placing the stethoscope at her ears, Paige glanced at him. "You have some explaining to do," she said quietly, before putting the flat, round end of it on Sophie's chest.

Fifteen minutes later, after what Garrett was sure was a thorough exam, Paige reached down into a basket on the floor and pulled out a children's picture book. "Do you like to read, Sophie?" she asked. A nod was Sophie's reply, and Paige handed her the book. "Your daddy and I are going to go out in the hall for a minute. If you need anything, all you have to do is jump down and open the door. We'll be right on the other side of it. Okay?"

When Sophie had nodded and opened her book, Garrett followed his sister into the hall, still reeling at someone using the word *daddy* when referring to him. "Well?"

"She appears to be healthy. Her vitals are good. Heartbeat is strong, lungs are clear, no cold or anything else going on. Of course I can't be completely sure without lab tests, but at this point in time, I don't see a reason for them, unless you want them done."

He shook his head. As soon as he could track down Shana, he'd know more. Lifting his gaze to his sister's, he brought up the one thing that had been bothering him the most. "She hasn't spoken."

Paige shrugged. "My best guess is that it isn't physical. Her hearing seems normal, as does everything else. She said 'Ah' when I asked her to, so it's nothing with her vocal cords. It may be that she just isn't ready to talk. Any clue why that would be?"

Knowing she was expecting an explanation, he told her what had happened, starting with the call from Tootie while he was having lunch. "If I'd known…"

"Apparently her mother didn't want you to know. Her loss. She doesn't sound very stable."

"She isn't." But that's all he would say. There wasn't any reason to tell his sister about a relationship that had ended five years before. Not unless there was something wrong with Sophie, and apparently there wasn't. Not physically, anyway.

Paige put her hand on his arm. "Is there anything else I can do to help?"

Garrett hoped what he was going to say next wouldn't come out sounding wrong, but he didn't have a choice. "I'd like to have a paternity test done."

Paige nodded, her expression serious. "I can arrange that for you."

"Good," he answered. "I'd appreciate it. Just let me know when and where."

"Do you have someone to watch her during the day?" she asked.

"That's next on my list of things to do."

"I'll be happy to help when I can, but all I have free is evenings and weekends. That won't help you during the day."

"I'll find someone." At least he hoped he would. He didn't know what types of day care were available in Desperation. He'd never needed to know.

"One more thing," Paige said. "As soon as you can, have Jules talk to her. This whole thing sounds terribly traumatic. I'm not all that surprised that she isn't talking."

"I will."

She gave him a quick hug. "You may not think so, but everything will work out. Give it time."

He thanked her, and then he retrieved Sophie and headed for home. They were a block away when he realized there might not be anything in his house for dinner. Too often he didn't think ahead and simply grabbed something at the café or at Lou's. He was going to have to learn to do some real shopping. Cooking, too. Not that he didn't know how, but cooking for one had never excited him, so he didn't do a lot of it.

He slowed to a stop when Vern Isley stepped out between two parked cars to cross the street. Even when the eightysomething gentleman was all the way to the other side of the street, Garrett remained stopped. He chuckled to himself. Where there's Vern, there's Esther.

Sure enough, Esther Watson stepped out between the same two cars and hurried across the street, several yards behind Vern. "One of these days…" Garrett said, the car now in motion again.

Glancing in his rearview mirror, he tried for a cheery voice. "You're in for a real treat, Sophie," he said, while making a U-turn at the end of the block. "I'm going to take you to the Chick-a-Lick Café for dinner. You can't ask for much better than that."

From the used booster seat that Tootie had managed to find and was now attached in the backseat, Sophie watched him. The sky was darkening as dusk began to settle in, but he could see his daughter's solemn expression. He hoped that would soon change. She'd come to him with a small suitcase, a battered teddy bear and a lot of questions that might or might not be answered. He had a lot of work to do, but he didn't have a clue where to begin.

Libby pulled into an empty parking spot at the sports park and shut off her engine. The view from her car made her smile. A dozen or so nine- and ten-year-olds, dressed in football pads and helmets, were gathered in a huddle in the middle of an unmarked, grassy field. She watched as they stacked their hands in a pile, then shouted, before breaking up the huddle and taking their places in the lineup.

It wasn't difficult to find her nine-year-old in the midst of the others. He was the one making encouraging signals to the others. It was only a practice, but Noah didn't let anything stop him from trying to inspire his fellow players with the will to win.

Leaning her head back against the seat, she closed her eyes. Life hadn't been a bed of roses since she and Noah had left Phoenix in the middle of the night barely eight months ago. Even so, it was better than it had promised to be if they'd stayed. Living in a small town in Oklahoma had never been a part of her plans, but nothing she *had* planned had worked out well. And she liked Desperation. Noah did, too. So she prayed they wouldn't have to leave, but neither did she count on staying.

A knock on her window jerked her out of her reverie, and she opened her eyes, then sat up with a smile.

"Hey, Mom," Noah said, peering into the car with his own smile.

She rolled down her window. "Is practice over?"

"Yeah, we're quitting early today." He looked around at the other boys, who were drifting away in twos and threes or climbing into cars with a parent or two. "I didn't expect you to be here, and I told Kirby we could hang out until you got here."

Libby hated disappointing her son more than anything, but it couldn't be helped. "I'm afraid not, honey," she told him. "I came to pick you up because I thought maybe we could stop at the Chick-a-Lick for dinner before I go to work."

His eyes lit up, then quickly dimmed, before he ducked his head. Without looking up at her, he asked, "I guess he can't come to the café with us?"

She couldn't help but feel disappointed. She'd thought he would be excited to have the chance to eat at the café. They so seldom were able to enjoy even the small things. But she'd worked the extra hours and had a few extra tips, so they could afford—

She stopped herself, suddenly realizing that she was having a pity party for herself, and her selfishness surprised her. How much could a nine-year-old boy eat, anyway? She knew the answer was that they could often be a bottomless pit, but it shouldn't matter.

"Sure, Kirby can come along, too," she said. She'd make up for the little extra somewhere along the way. Giving Noah the chance to spend time with his friend was worth it.

She heard a shout, and Noah turned to look. She looked, too. A fancy sports car had pulled up, and Kirby was headed for it, waving at Noah as he walked toward it.

"It's okay," Noah said. "Looks like Mac got here early, too." He turned to his mom. "So we're going to the Chick-a-Lick?" he asked, without a hint of disappointment.

Libby looked at her watch. They had less than two hours before she had to be at work.

Just enough time, if they hurried, to enjoy dinner at the café. "I worked a few extra hours this morning," she explained. "Get in. You can order anything you want."

"Cool."

She laughed as he circled the car and opened the back door to get in. How did she get so lucky to have such a good kid?

When Noah was settled in the backseat, she drove the two blocks to the café, thinking about how things might have been. Before she'd divorced Noah's father, there'd been enough money to take an entire boys' football team to a fancy restaurant—after every practice. In fact, Noah's third birthday party had been held at Chase Field. More than one hundred guests had attended, most of them friends and business associates of her ex-husband and his family. She often wondered if Noah remembered it, but she'd never asked. It no longer mattered. They weren't the same people they were then.

Those were the times Libby didn't want to think about, so she concentrated on parking only a few spaces down from the café. Luckily the dinner crowd hadn't yet arrived. "Any idea what you're going to order?" she asked, as they stepped up onto the sidewalk.

"That depends," he answered.

"Really? On what?" She reached for the door to the café to open it, but Noah beat her to it. Surprised, she thanked him with a smile as she passed inside.

"*You* know."

She did, and it hurt her heart and her pride. Noah rarely complained when there wasn't enough money left over at the end of the month to do something special. It was the price they paid for safety. She'd done her best to explain it to him when they left Phoenix, and he must have understood at least part of it.

She leaned down and spoke in a quiet voice. "You can have anything on the menu."

He looked up at her as she straightened, a sparkle in his dark brown eyes. "Anything?"

The café was more than half full, and she nodded to answer him while they made their way to one of the smaller booths in the back. She'd just slid into the booth when Darla appeared to take their order.

"It's good to see you two," Darla greeted them. "Would you like menus?"

"Please," Libby asked, winking at Noah.

Darla handed them each a menu. "I'll be back in a couple of minutes with your water and to take your orders."

After Darla walked away, Libby noticed that

Noah was propping his menu on the table and apparently studying it closely. "Everything looks good, doesn't it?" she asked, looking at her own.

"Yeah."

Darla returned within minutes and took their orders. "Was that okay?" he asked when she was gone.

"Perfectly okay." Libby glanced at her watch, making certain they still had plenty of time before she had to take Noah to his day care provider and get herself to work.

She asked about school and listened as Noah gave her a rundown of his day. Getting him to talk about school had always been easy. All he needed was a nudge, and he was ready to share. He was explaining something that had happened in gym class when Darla arrived with their order.

"It looks great," Noah said, looking up at Darla with a grin.

"Then we'll hope it tastes as good as it looks, won't we?" she asked, winking at his mom.

"Oh, I know it will."

Darla laughed and patted his shoulder. "He's a keeper."

They were well into enjoying their meal when Libby looked up to see Garrett entering the café with Sophie, who still held tight to her teddy bear. She smiled when he looked her way and was surprised when dad and daughter headed toward them.

Garrett stopped at their booth, with Sophie beside him. "If I'd known you were going to be here, we could have planned to have dinner together," he said.

Libby noticed that the panic hadn't completely left his eyes. "Last-minute plans," she explained.

He glanced around the room, and then shifted from one foot to the other. "Well, we'd better let you both finish eating."

Before he could move away, she touched his arm. "I don't think you've met my son. Noah, this is Garrett Miles."

"Hi," Noah greeted him with a small smile.

"And that's his daughter, Sophie," she added.

"Hi, Sophie."

Sophie grinned at Noah, but said nothing.

"She's…uh…a little shy," Garrett said, with a glance at Libby. "We stopped to see Paige."

Libby hoped his sister had found the girl in good physical condition. "How did that go?"

"Good," he said, although it sounded forced. When she didn't reply, he blew out a short breath. "She said to give it some time. And to talk to Jules."

"But everything else is okay, right?"

He nodded, and his smile was more relaxed. "Everything is okay. But we should let you finish your dinner," he added, taking a step back.

She looked at her watch and then at her son. "We should probably be on our way. I still have a full shift to work tonight."

Garrett moved away from the booth as Libby gathered her things. "I'm glad we ran into you," he said. "And, Noah, the next time we see each other, I want to hear a little about that football team you play on."

Noah, who was scooting out of his seat, looked up, a wide smile on his face. "You bet!"

Libby was surprised he had remembered about her son's football team. She'd only mentioned it once, so it was especially nice of him to say something. "Enjoy your meal," she told them, as she turned toward the cash register.

"Bye, Mr. Miles," Noah said, following her. "Bye, Sophie."

Garrett waved, and so did Sophie, and Libby imagined the hard time he was probably having. She wished him well. Being a single parent wasn't easy. Being a parent of a child who might have undergone some kind of trauma was even harder. He definitely had his work cut out for him.

After paying for their dinner, Libby and Noah stepped outside and walked to their car. Driving toward Noah's day care provider's house, she rolled down her window and inhaled deeply, breathing in the warm, early September evening.

"I like it a lot here, don't you, Mom?" Noah asked from the backseat.

"It's a nice town, yes."

"Mr. Miles is a nice man."

Libby glanced in her rearview mirror, wondering what Noah might be up to. But the sun had already set and shadows kept her from seeing his face. "Yes, he's nice. He comes into Lou's two or three times a week."

"Are you good friends with him?"

She nearly laughed. "No, not good friends," she answered, as honestly as she could. She wasn't quite sure what to call her odd relationship with Garrett. "Just friends, I guess."

Silence settled over the car, and she thought about how well they were doing in Desperation. Noah liked school and had made several new friends. She didn't mind her job at the tavern. It didn't pay badly, and the tips were often more than satisfying. They did all right.

But she knew it might not be a forever thing. Anything could happen, and she had to be careful. Thanks to an underground group, she'd managed to get Noah and herself out of Phoenix without being followed by her ex-husband. They had new names, new identities, new everything, and she hoped it would all continue to work out well. But in the back of her mind, there were always the memories of the abuse she'd endured from her ex-husband and the fear she'd had that he might do the same to their son. And maybe, just maybe he had.

Garrett unlocked the front door, nudged it open with his shoulder and stepped inside to flip on the light switch. "Did you like your dinner?" he asked, as Sophie followed closely behind him. He looked back to see her nodding, a small, shy smile turning up the corners of her mouth.

He walked to the TV and turned it on, remembering that there were a few channels that broadcast nothing but cartoons all day and night. Maybe that would keep Sophie entertained until he could get his head together and figure out what he needed to do next.

"How's this?" he asked, as a big gray cat chased a little mouse under a table on the screen. She nodded, and he pointed to the sofa, while grabbing a small pillow for her. "You can sit there, if you want to."

She took the pillow he handed her, then climbed onto the sofa and curled up in the corner, her attention glued on the cat-and-mouse chase on TV. Before he had a chance to wonder what he needed to do next, the phone rang.

"I should have invited you over for supper," Paige said with an accompanying sigh, when he answered it. "Is everything going okay?"

"I realized I didn't really have anything here for us to eat, so we went to the café. I think she enjoyed it." He could see her from his spot near the kitchen doorway. "She's watching TV right now."

"She's probably exhausted," Paige answered, "considering everything that she's gone through today. Maybe she'd like to go to bed?"

Garrett hadn't even thought about how everything might look from Sophie's point of view. What kind of father was he? "Yeah, you're right. I'll get her into bed, and then make a list of the things I need to do tomorrow."

"Maybe a warm bath would help."

His first thought was to answer that she

knew he preferred showers, but then he realized she was referring to a bath for Sophie. "Yeah, good idea."

"Give her a kiss for me," Paige said, before wishing him luck and saying goodbye.

After hanging up the phone, he walked to the living room, where Sophie was still focused on the antics of the cat and the mouse that wouldn't be caught. "Sophie?"

She turned her attention to him slowly.

"Would you like to take a bath?"

It was several seconds before she nodded, and she didn't move from the corner of the sofa.

"I'll go fill the tub for you, okay?" When she nodded again, this time without hesitation, he felt better. "Okay, you can watch the cartoon while I do that, and I'll let you know when it's ready."

After receiving another nod, he started for the bathroom, but changed course and walked across the hall to retrieve the one suitcase she'd brought with her. He placed it on the bed and quickly went through the few things that were in it, finally pulling out a pair of well-worn pajamas. It definitely appeared that in addition to needing to do some grocery shopping, he also needed to do some clothes shopping. She'd come with so very little, and he didn't even know where to start. He'd never given any thought to being a father or to how difficult it might be.

Pushing the pity thoughts away, he moved on to the bathroom, where he ran a warm bath, then went into the living room to let her know it was ready. "Sophie?" he said, taking care to speak softly so he wouldn't scare her. She looked up at him, and he smiled. "Your bath is ready."

He followed her down the hall to the bathroom, where she went inside and shut the door, leaving him standing outside. He wished he'd had some bubble bath to add, but Paige must have taken any she had with her when she moved out a few months earlier. One more item to add to his list of things to get.

Leaning against the wall, he waited, and it wasn't as long as he'd thought it would be before Sophie emerged from the bathroom, dressed in the pajamas he'd left for her.

Without saying a word, she walked to the bedroom that had been Paige's and peeked inside. "It's yours," he told her. "I know it doesn't look anything like a little girl's room, but we'll fix that real soon. It was my sister's room when she lived here."

Sophie's hazel eyes were wide and unreadable, but she nodded slowly. Her head turned toward the big bed, and then back again.

It was his turn to nod. "Go ahead, climb into bed and I'll tuck you in." He suddenly smiled at the memory of his mother saying the same to him. Feeling a little easier, not to mention nostalgic, he waited until she'd crawled onto the bed and scooted under the covers before approaching. "Up to your chin?" he asked, taking the top edge of the blanket in his fingers.

But Sophie wasn't paying attention. Her gaze darted around the room, as if she were looking for something. At first, he wasn't sure what it might be, and he suspected Sophie wouldn't suddenly speak up and tell him what the problem was, so he looked around, too. And then it dawned on him.

"Your teddy bear?" When she nodded, he felt a knot in his chest ease. "You left it on the sofa. I'll get it and will be right back." He barely waited for her nod before he turned for the door and hurried to the living room, where he scooped up the tattered teddy bear and returned to her room.

She hadn't moved an inch. The big bed seemed to swallow her, and he made another mental note, along with the others, to find a smaller bed for her. When he handed her the teddy bear, he noticed that the relief on her face turned to joy. Apparently something was right. Finally.

After making sure she was comfortable, he brushed his lips lightly on her cheek. He felt her still, and when he moved away, she was watching him closely. He wasn't sure what to make of it.

"I'll be down the hall in my office," he told her, switching on a small bedside lamp. "If you need anything, just come get me, okay?"

She nodded, her face solemn. Unsure if he should leave her alone, he finally moved toward the door. "Good night, Sophie."

He hadn't been in his office for five minutes when he thought he heard crying. Stepping carefully out into the hall, he listened closely. His heart ached at the sound of whimpers and soft sobs coming from her room, but he wasn't sure what to do. Should he go in and assure her that everything would be all right? It might be a promise he couldn't keep.

Instead of going in to try to soothe her—something he was certain he would fail at—he returned to his office and put away his things. A few minutes later, he listened at her door. The crying had stopped, and he suspected she might have fallen asleep. Opening the door as quietly as possible, he looked inside.

The soft glow of the lamp lit her small features, and he was again immediately reminded of his sister. Was it wishful thinking? Did he *really* want to do this? Did he want to be a father?

The thought of raising a small child terrified him. He'd seen what parents could do to their children. He'd chosen long ago not to father a child. And yet it had happened.

He'd have the paternity test done. He needed proof that she was his. Not only for himself, but for the future and whatever it might bring.

But most of all, he wondered if he was going to screw this up. The thought chased everything else from his mind. He searched, but he couldn't find an answer.

Chapter Three

Libby drummed her fingers on the steering wheel, wondering if she'd ever find a place to park. The last thing she wanted or needed was to be late for Noah's football game, but she hadn't expected there to be so many people attending Desperation's Fall Festival. She'd forgotten how people in town turned out for all of the town's celebrations, but then she'd only been in town for about eight months. It all had her wondering what Christmas would be like.

Finally finding a spot that was so far away she could've saved herself the trouble and walked from home, she parked and stepped out of the car. "I should be used to it," she muttered under her breath as she began walking toward the sound of the music in the distance. "After all, I'm on my feet all night."

As she approached the carnival that had been set up around the baseball field, the music grew louder, and she could see the top of a Ferris wheel. The closer she got, the more people of all ages and sizes she saw milling around the area. To her surprise, she recognized more than she thought she would have. Maybe she wasn't such a stranger in Desperation, after all.

But maybe that wasn't such a good idea, she thought, making her way through the crowd. She couldn't really get close to anyone. Not for a while, at least. Not until she felt comfortable being who she'd become. Who she'd *had* to become.

"Libby?"

Pulled from going down a memory path she really shouldn't, she turned to see the secretary from the grade school. "Hi, Sadie."

"I've been keeping a lookout for you," Sadie said, joining her. "I was afraid you might miss Noah's game."

Libby shook her head and smiled. "I'll miss the fireworks tonight, but not his game this morning."

"That's the important thing."

"I was beginning to wonder if he was going to tell me he didn't want me to be here," Libby admitted with a soft laugh. "He forbade me to come to practices."

Sadie laughed, too. "They can get strange at this age. I went through the same thing with Kevin's two older brothers, so I guess I'm used to it."

Libby appreciated Sadie's friendship. They weren't close friends, but Sadie had been a big help with enrolling Noah in school, which had been well into the second semester. It might have been a nightmare, but Sadie had made it painless.

"I didn't realize this Fall Festival thing was so popular," Libby admitted.

"Any excuse to get out and have a good time. Maybe it's to make up for the name of our town," Sadie suggested. "Whatever, we do know how to throw a party."

Libby definitely agreed.

Now in the midst of the carnival, she looked around to see the smiling faces of her neighbors and people she'd only seen once or twice. Everyone seemed to be enjoying the perfect fall day. Everyone except Letha Adkins, who was glaring at her, as usual.

"Don't let her bother you," Sadie said, leaning closer. "I've never seen the woman without a frown. Unless she was needling someone."

Libby simply nodded. She knew she wasn't popular among at least a few people in town. After all, she did work at Lou's. For some that meant she didn't measure up. It didn't bother her much. She wasn't in Desperation to win a popularity contest. She only wanted a place to live where she hoped to keep her son and herself safe. Besides, most of the rest of the people she'd met were nice.

They left the carnival behind and approached the football field, where two small sets of bleachers held several parents and friends of the young players. As they drew nearer, she spied Garrett among them. His daughter was at his side, and Libby wondered who they'd come to watch play.

Sadie introduced Libby to her husband, who was sitting on the row just below Garrett. When Sadie invited her to join them, she did hesitate for a brief moment, but she didn't want to sit alone, so she accepted.

As she settled next to Sadie, she turned to say hello to Garrett. "I wasn't aware you were a peewee football fan."

"Baseball is more my game," he answered,

"but Noah mentioned he had a game today, so I thought I'd come. Hope that's all right."

She was surprised. "He did? Of course it's okay," she hurried to assure him. There was no reason why he couldn't be there, too, but Noah hadn't mentioned it.

Refusing to let something so simple bother her, she smiled at his daughter. "Hi, Sophie."

When the little girl returned the smile but said nothing, Libby glanced at Garrett, who shrugged and shook his head. "So how much do you know about football?" he asked.

Libby nearly answered that she had a much older brother, but stopped herself. "Not nearly as much as I need to, considering my son is playing."

Sophie, who'd been watching them closely, patted the bench beside her. It was clear to Libby that it was an invitation to sit next to her. With Sadie busy talking to her husband, Libby didn't think it would matter if she moved up to sit with the little girl. Even though spending time with Garrett might not be a good idea, she didn't want to disappoint his daughter.

"I think it's about to start," Libby said, as the teams began to line up on the field for the kickoff and she settled next to Sophie.

"That's Kirby MacGregor, Mac and Nikki's boy, who's doing the kicking," Garrett explained.

"He's one of Noah's friends," she said, without taking her eyes off the field. "He didn't mention they weren't on the same team."

Garrett chuckled softly. "Friendly adversaries for the duration of the game?"

"That's probably it," Libby answered, hoping she could relax a little.

"There are teams in some of the other towns around here, so it isn't as if they don't have the chance to play teams with players they don't know. But I heard there were enough boys interested to make up two teams. That makes it nice. More of them actually get a chance to play."

Libby nodded and straightened as the football on the little stand connected with Kirby's foot and went sailing through the air. Boys of all sizes scattered on the field, and before long, she'd become so engrossed in the game, she forgot about Garrett.

"You must know more about football than you let on," he said, jerking her attention from the game.

"I attended a few football games when I was young." She hoped her answer wasn't so vague that he'd start asking questions, and she shouted, "Go, blue," as one of the players on Noah's team ran down the length of the field. Not only was she excited when the boy scored a touchdown, but she was relieved that the attention was taken off what school she'd attended. The less she had to make up, the better.

Within minutes, the game ended and the bleachers were spilling over with excited fans and players. "I guess your first game was about as good as it can get," Garrett remarked to Noah when the boy joined them.

"No kidding!" Noah replied, laughing. He looked at Libby, his expression hopeful. "Would it be okay if I stay and ride some of the rides? I have enough money for a couple."

"Maybe I can give you a little more," she answered, "but I'll have to pick you up before I go to work."

Garrett put his hand on Noah's shoulder, but spoke to Libby. "I'll take care of his tickets, if he'll ride a couple of rides with Sophie. She dragged me to the Ferris wheel earlier, but I told her we needed to wait until after Noah's game."

Libby looked at Noah, who glanced at Kirby before answering. "Yeah, sure," he said with a shrug.

"What time do you have to be at work?" Garrett asked.

"In about four hours."

"Why don't you stick around for a while?" Garrett suggested. "Unless you have something you need to do, that is. It's almost noon. We can grab a bite at one of the food booths."

Not sure that spending more time with Garrett than she had already was a good idea, Libby glanced at Sophie. The silent begging in the girl's eyes was enough to make her give Garrett's suggestion another chance. When she looked quickly at Noah to see what he might think, he nodded. There wouldn't be any begging off.

"Sure," she answered, unable to say no to all of them. "I have some time, and we all need to eat, right?"

"Right," Garrett answered, smiling. "Let's hit the rides first."

Libby nodded, though her heart skipped a beat. All it took was looking up into Garrett's soft gray eyes, and she knew she was heading for trouble. And she'd already had enough of that for a lifetime.

"No, really, I don't want to ride," Libby protested.

But Garrett didn't like the idea of leaving her out of the fun. "You can go with Noah and

I'll go with Sophie. Or you can go with both of them, and I'll wait here."

She took a step back, away from the line at the Ferris wheel, her chin at a defiant angle. "Absolutely not."

He didn't want to pressure her any more. He'd railroaded her into coming with him and Sophie, and he felt bad about it. But it wasn't for him. It was for his daughter. Considering that even after almost a week he still felt completely at a loss at what to do or say, he needed someone to just be around. Noah and Libby were the perfect ones.

"Okay, you don't have to ride," he said. "Noah, come with me. Let's get you a ride bracelet." He turned to Libby. "Do you mind watching Sophie for a minute?"

Her face softened and she looked down at Sophie with a smile. "Of course not, but you don't need to—"

Garrett stopped listening as he put his arm around Noah's shoulders and led him to the ticket booth. He wasn't willing to argue with Libby or make up excuses as to why he should pay for Noah's rides. He had the money, she didn't. And she was helping him by just spending time with them.

"Mom's not comfortable when people do

things for her," Noah said, while Garrett handed over the money to the woman in the booth.

"Then she'll just have to not be comfortable," Garrett replied. "Put your hand up there so the lady can put the bracelet on you."

When they were finished, they started back toward the Ferris wheel. Noah held up his arm. "I'll pay you back for this."

Garrett stopped dead in his tracks. "You're just like your mom, aren't you?"

At first, it appeared that Noah was going to argue. Instead, he ducked his head, shuffled the toe of one shoe in the grass and then looked up with an embarrassed grin. "Like mother, like son."

"Do me a favor, will you?" Garrett asked. Noah nodded. "Forget about it. I'm doing this for Sophie, not for you or your mom. And you can tell your mom that later, if you think it will help."

Noah nodded. "It might."

Feeling a little better, but still determined not to let these two people think he was helping, he started for the Ferris wheel. He liked Libby. He wasn't going to deny that. But with a four-year-old daughter now in his life, he sure didn't need to even think about having a woman in it, too. He had enough to handle.

"Everything okay?" he asked Libby when he and Noah joined her and Sophie.

"Just fine," Libby answered. "You got the bracelet?" she asked Noah. When he nodded, she looked up at Garrett, stubborn determination in the set of her jaw.

"Forget it, Libby," he said, before she could utter a sound. "Please."

"It's okay, Mom," Noah said quickly. "I already told him I'd pay him back."

Libby visibly relaxed. "All right, then."

Garrett bit his lower lip to keep from smiling. "Okay, so let's get this ride thing organized. Are the three of us going to fit okay?"

Noah looked at Sophie, and then at Garrett. "I think so, but... Mom?"

"You'll all fit. Looks like it's your turn on the next stop."

The four of them watched as the wheel rotated down toward them, slowing to a halt. Two high school girls climbed out of the seat, and Garrett turned to take Sophie's hand. The three of them climbed into the roomy seat, Sophie in the middle, between them.

When the safety bar clicked, Libby waved and announced, "I think I'll go scout out some lunch possibilities."

The operator stepped away and pulled a

lever. The wheel began to move. Beside him, Garrett felt Sophie stiffen. "It's okay," he told her. Her eyes were as big as dinner plates, and he took her small hand in his. "We'll stop going backward when we get up to the top. See the ball field where Noah was playing earlier?"

"Don't be scared," Noah said. "Take a deep breath and close your eyes, if you are. When you get used to it, then you can open them."

Garrett watched as she did as Noah instructed. After they stopped several times to let off old riders and take on new ones, and then made two complete circles, she'd relaxed. When she finally opened her eyes, there was a slight smile playing on her lips.

"Better?" he asked.

She looked up at him with a real smile and nodded.

For the rest of the ride, he and Noah pointed out different things to her, and by the time the ride was over, she was giggling. Garrett couldn't remember hearing anything so beautiful.

When their ride was over and they were on solid ground again, Garrett looked around, but didn't see Libby. "Do you see your mom?" he asked Noah.

Noah looked around, too. "No. Should I go look for her?"

Before Garrett could answer, he felt some-one touch his arm. When he turned around, he saw Hettie Lambert, the great-granddaughter of the town's founder, and her friend Aggie Clayborne.

"I heard you have a little girl," Hettie said, smiling down at Sophie. "What a cutie!"

Having received the results of the pater-nity test the day before, there was no doubt left in Garrett's mind that Sophie was his. He felt proud. He felt scared. News had traveled quickly in Desperation, as he had expected it would, and most folks knew that he was now a single father. He wasn't surprised that Het-tie had come to be introduced to Sophie, nor was he going to disappoint her.

"Thank you," he answered. "This is my daughter, Sophie."

"She looks just like your sister," Aggie said. "Definitely a family resemblance."

"And she's just adorable," Hettie added. Bending down, she touched Sophie's cheek. "Welcome to Desperation, Sophie. I hope you like it here. Are you having a good time today?"

Garrett knew there'd be no verbal response from his daughter. "She's a little shy, Hettie."

Hettie straightened. "Oh, that's all right. Don't you worry about it, Sophie. Aggie and I are just two old ladies with nothing better to do than watch people having a good time at this carnival." She turned to Garrett. "I'd like to talk to you about the new zoning, if you have a couple of minutes."

"Of course." He was always willing to give Hettie all the time she needed for anything. She didn't hold a position on the council and never had, but she watched over the town as if it were her child and kept abreast of everything and everyone, making sure nothing and no one were ever in need.

He listened patiently to her concerns about the new zoning for a convenience store on the outskirts of town, answered her questions and then did his best to explain how he expected the council to vote when the time came.

"That makes me feel much easier," Hettie said. "Thank you for taking the time, Garrett. I know this isn't the time or place, but Aggie and I have been talking it over, and we both thought our best course was to come to you."

After assuring both of them that he was always willing to help, they thanked him again and moved on. Content that he'd told them all that he could, he smiled and started to walk away. He'd taken no more than three steps, when he looked down and realized Sophie wasn't with him. He turned back, trying to convince himself that she was standing where he'd just been. But she wasn't. In fact, he didn't see her anywhere in the immediate area, as he frantically looked around for her.

What had he done? His heart pounded as he quickly surveyed the area again, hoping she'd simply been hidden behind someone for a moment. But not only did he not see Sophie, he realized that Noah wasn't anywhere nearby, either.

Could Sophie have gone with Noah, wherever he went? Garrett thought it might be possible. He hadn't spent much more than five minutes with Hettie, so neither of them could have gone far. So again he searched, hoping to catch sight of the two children and afraid to go too far away.

But his heart took a nosedive when he spied Noah walking toward him, with Libby not far behind. "Is Sophie with you?" he called to them.

Noah turned to look at his mother, then both shook their heads. "She was standing right there," he said, pointing to the spot where Garrett had stood talking to Hettie and Aggie.

Garrett had felt panic before. In fact, a week ago, when he'd discovered Sophie for the first time in his office and had read the letter her mother had written, announcing that Sophie was all his, he thought he'd never felt so scared in his life.

He'd been wrong.

Libby said something to Noah, who hurried away, then she approached Garrett. "The first thing you need to do is calm down," she said, her voice quiet and even.

"How can I calm down?" he asked, raking his hand through his hair. "I've lost my daughter, Libby. My little girl. What kind of father does that?"

"A normal one," she answered. "Where were you the last time you saw her?" she asked.

He pointed to the spot near the Ferris wheel where he'd been talking to Hettie. "Right over there."

She slipped her hand around his arm and steered him in that direction. "How long has she been gone?"

The panic only seemed to get worse. "I don't know. Ten minutes, maybe? I introduced her to Hettie and Aggie, and when Hettie and I finished talking city council business, I realized Sophie wasn't standing there anymore." He looked around the area, silently praying that he'd see Sophie. "I can't believe I've lost my child! I can't believe I wasn't paying attention." He stared at Libby, his eyes stinging. "What kind of father would do that?"

"These kind of things happen to the best of us, Garrett. It'll be all right," Libby insisted. When he started to tell her how wrong she was, she stopped him. "Guess what, Garrett? You're as human as the rest of us. Parent or not, none of us is perfect. Sophie will be found, and she'll be fine. She couldn't have gone far, and I'm sure—"

"Garrett?"

He turned toward the voice, and his knees nearly buckled. Tucker O'Brien, one of Desperation's sheriff deputies, walked toward him, holding Sophie's hand. "I think this little one belongs to you," Tucker said, when they reached Garrett and Libby.

Garrett dropped to his knees in front of Sophie and scooped her into his arms, hugging her and silently swearing he'd never let her out of his sight again, not even for one second.

He looked up at Tucker. "Where did you find her?"

"Well," Tucker said, grinning at Noah, who was now standing with Libby, "if you'd loosen that grip you have on her, you might be able to figure that out yourself."

Garrett stared at him. "What?" Understanding quickly dawned and he loosened his hold on Sophie, who moved back a little. It was then that he noticed there was a lump of something between them.

"Noah found her over by the game booths, staring at that teddy bear, so he threw darts at balloons until he ran out of money. The guy running the booth said he couldn't stand the brokenhearted look on Noah's face when his money was gone and no balloons were broken, or the tears in Sophie's eyes, so he gave them the bear."

Sophie moved back a little more and held up the toy.

"Well, I'll be," Garrett said, and had to clear his throat. "I guess you have yourself a new teddy bear."

Libby stood at the sink in the tiny duplex apartment she shared with her son. Lou had sent her home early from working an additional Sunday shift. She was tired and her back hurt, but she wouldn't leave the few dirty dishes until tomorrow. There was little worse than waking to a messy kitchen sink.

"It's time for bed, Noah," she announced, without turning around.

"Aw, Mom, can't I stay up a little longer?"

Libby chuckled to herself. If he hadn't tried that, she would've known he was sick. "Fifteen minutes."

"Twenty?"

She turned around and looked at him over the open counter that separated the kitchen from the living room. "You're wasting time."

He looked up from the miniature race track he was playing with and grinned. "I know."

Wiping her wet hands on a towel, she joined him to watch two small cars race along the intricate layout of the track. "Is it working okay now?"

He nodded. "Better than ever. You can fix just about anything, can't you?"

"Oh, I don't know about that."

"Mr. Miles is a nice man," Noah said, taking her by surprise.

She thought of how Garrett had been blindsided when he learned he was a father, and then how distraught he'd been the day before when Sophie had disappeared. Swallowing a sigh, she smoothed Noah's dark hair with her fingers. "Put the cars away and get into your pajamas."

"Can I leave the track set up?"

Surveying the floor where the track twisted and turned around and under the worn furniture, she didn't have the heart to say no. He'd worked hard to get it set up just the way he wanted it.

"Sure," she answered. "I don't have to be at work tomorrow until later. You'll have some time to play with it after school and football practice if you want to."

Noah jumped up and threw his arms around her. "Thanks, Mom. You're the best."

"Well, I try," she answered as she always did.

She watched him pocket the two race cars and start down the short hallway to his bedroom. Noah was a blessing, and she really did try hard to be a good mom. She wanted to give him the best of everything, especially the things he deserved. But on a waitress's salary—

The buzz of the doorbell cut off her thoughts.

"I'll get it!" Noah raced back down the hallway and nearly beat her to the door.

"Better let me," she told him, and moved to open it. They didn't have many visitors, and she couldn't imagine who would be stopping by. There were reasons to be cautious, and sometimes Noah forgot.

Opening the door enough to see who was on the other side, she was surprised to find Garrett standing on her doorstep, Sophie at his side.

He held up a paper sack. "I brought ice cream."

Libby didn't understand and thought she might have heard wrong. "Ice cream?"

"I wanted to thank you both for helping me yesterday," he said with a shrug.

"There's no need to—" But the look on his face told her that wouldn't float with him. "Noah was just on his way to bed."

But her son slipped under her arm, opening the door wider to stand in front of her. "Hey, Sophie," he greeted the little girl, and then looked up at Garrett, grinning.

Garrett looked at him and returned the grin. "Do you think your mom will give you a bedtime reprieve?"

Libby silently moaned. How could she say no? Placing her hand on Noah's shoulder, she sighed. "This time it's okay," she said, glancing at Garrett and hoping he understood it was a one-time-only thing and wouldn't be repeated. "Go put your cars in your room, wash your hands and you can have some ice cream."

She had to admit that the idea of dessert

sounded yummy. It wasn't something they often enjoyed. Just keeping a roof over their heads and nutritious food in their stomachs tended to stretch her waitress's salary, even when tips were good. Ice cream was a treat.

"Come on in," she told Garrett, opening the door wider as Noah headed for his room.

Garrett and Sophie stepped inside the apartment. "Will it keep him up too late?" he asked. "I mean, I hadn't thought of that. I guess I should have."

Libby shrugged her shoulders and pointed to the table near the narrow kitchen. "Which is better, more sleep or the chance to have ice cream?"

Grinning, he set the sack on the table. "I know what I'd pick, but you're the expert."

"Ha!" She scooped up the pile of bills in plain sight on the table and turned around to stuff them next to the toaster on the counter. "If only it was that easy."

Noting how tense and nervous she suddenly felt, she forced herself to relax. She picked up the sack and looked inside it to find several containers of ice cream and a variety of toppings. Ready to tell him he shouldn't have, she was saved by Noah's return.

"Let me see your hands," she told him.

Checking them for dirt of any kind, she approved. "Would you get us all bowls and spoons, please?"

"I'll help," Garrett said.

Libby pulled a tall stool from the corner and positioned it at the table. Picking up Sophie, she was surprised when the little girl put her arms around her neck and pressed her cheek to Libby's. "It's been kind of hard, hasn't it?" Libby whispered to her, her heart squeezing, before setting Sophie on the stool.

Garrett and Noah delivered the bowls and spoons, while Libby opened the ice cream, then they all took their seats. As they enjoyed the sundaes they built, Libby listened to the conversation between Garrett and her son, saying very little herself. She'd thought she was impressed with the man before, but he had a way with Noah that most men didn't. For someone who claimed to have no idea of how to relate to children, he was doing a pretty good job of it. She was pleased to see Noah enjoying himself. She only hoped he didn't enjoy it too much. Kids had a way of latching on to someone and not understanding that it wouldn't work out for the adults.

Garrett was a nice guy. She liked him, liked taking with him. It made her feel…worthwhile.

But she knew they could never—ever—go any further than just being friends. He was an attorney, and she had learned the hard way not to trust the court system. At one time she had, but the courts had failed her eight months ago, and she'd had to find another way. That way wasn't legal, but it was the only way she could be assured that Noah would be safe.

She'd placed her life and her son's in the hands of people who she only knew by their first names, and had ended up in Desperation, Oklahoma. The running had ended, but the hiding never would.

Chapter Four

As Libby waited on several of the regular customers, out of the corner of her eye she saw Garrett enter Lou's and head for his usual table. She hadn't seen or heard from him since he'd stopped by with the ice cream, and she hoped it was a sign that everything was going well with Sophie.

"Anything else I can get you?" she asked the men at the table. When they all shook their heads, she hurried to fill their order. As soon as they had their drinks, she headed toward Garrett. She suspected he would want his usual cup of coffee, and she was eager to hear how he was adjusting to parenthood.

"How's the new dad?" she asked when she reached his table.

He looked up with a weary, yet satisfied smile. "Wishing kids came with instructions."

She laughed, knowing exactly how he felt, and also knowing that it was a wish that would never be granted. "I'll just bet you do. But you've obviously survived the first couple of weeks." She laughed again when he snorted. "So how's Sophie doing? Is she talking yet?"

Shaking his head, he looked down, his hands clasped on the table in front of him. "I called Jules O'Brien, since she's a psychologist, but learned she's out of town. Thanks to Tanner, I was able to get in touch with her. She said there's no way of knowing what's causing Sophie's silence, but to give her time."

"She's probably right. And if you don't see any progress at all, I'm sure Jules will be happy to see and evaluate Sophie when she returns."

His eyebrows lifted. "You sound like you know a lot about this kind of thing."

"It's from being a mother, I guess," she said with a shrug of her shoulders. Those psychology classes she took in college helped, too, but she didn't mention them to Garrett. The less he knew about her, the better. They were friends.

Nothing more. And that's the way it would stay. It had to.

"How did you manage an evening out?" she asked. "Most parents—especially new ones—don't have that luxury. Did you lock her in a closet?" she teased.

Garrett's chuckle sent shivers of warmth through her. "Having a sister who's a doctor and childless—at least for a while—can be an advantage," he said. "Sophie is spending the evening with Paige and Tucker."

"And I'll bet they're enjoying it."

"For now," he said, his expression thoughtful. And then his mouth turned up in a smile of joy. "You should see Sophie's room. Every spare minute Paige and Tucker have had, they've been working on it. A complete make-over, Paige calls it."

"How nice of them! What does Sophie think of it?"

"She seems to like it. She was right there to watch it all, and Paige got as much input from her as she could. Of course, if Sophie had told us what she wanted, it might have been easier, but…"

Libby didn't miss the sad note in his voice or the worried creases between his eyes, and she placed her hand on his shoulder. "It'll work out." Realizing what she'd done, she pulled away and reached for the pencil from behind her ear. "So what can I—"

"Libby!"

She turned toward the voice and saw Lou only a few feet away, his scowl deep. "Be right back," she told Garrett. Under her breath as she walked away, she quietly muttered, "I hope."

"You need to do something," Lou said, his ham-size hands fisted on the white apron hanging from his hips. "I told her you were workin'."

When Libby was closer, she realized that not only was Janet Barkin, her day care provider there, but so was Noah. No wonder Lou was angry. Children weren't allowed in the tavern.

"What's wrong?" she asked Janet.

"It's just gotten to be too much," Janet said. "I just can't have him there every night. I want a normal life."

"You've got to get the boy out of here," Lou said, as if nothing else was happening.

"We need to step outside," Libby told Janet.

"I thought this would work out for us," Janet said as they finally stepped out into the cool night air. "But Randy is changing to first shift, and he won't be gone nights. I just can't have Noah there, and you traipsing in at all hours to pick him up. I—I'm sorry, but that's the way it is."

Libby understood. She'd known that finding someone to watch over Noah while she worked such odd hours would be difficult. Finding any kind of child care in Desperation was difficult.

With a sigh, she patted Janet's shoulder. "It's all right. I understand. I'll just have to find something else." If only she could!

The door opened, and Lou stepped outside. "You're going to have to take the boy home. He can't stay here. You know that." Nodding, Libby ducked her head, her eyes burning with unshed tears. If she couldn't find someone to watch after Noah, she'd lose her job. If that happened, she have to leave Desperation, and that was something she really didn't want to do. She liked the town and the people, even though she didn't have any close friends.

"I don't want to let you go, Libby," Lou continued. "You're a good worker and the customers like you. But I can't have your kid coming in here, and I can't have you runnin' off because of him, when I need you here the most. I gotta tell ya that if you leave now…" He shook his bald head.

She didn't have a choice. She had to take Noah home and stay there with him. It was still early, and she was scheduled to work until closing, which was well after midnight, but she had nowhere to leave Noah.

Swallowing the lump of tears that were threatening, she nodded and looked up at Lou. "I'll pick up my check on Monday."

Lou's face softened. "Maybe you can find somebody else to watch your boy? Or maybe he can get along on his own? If there's a neighbor close by—"

"He's only nine." She tugged at the towel at her waist. "But thanks, anyway. I'll just get my things and—"

The door opened again, and Garrett walked out. "What's going on?" he asked, looking from Libby to Lou.

Lou studied him with narrowed eyes. "You playin' lawyer tonight?"

Garrett shook his head. "No, just trying to find out what's going on."

Lou jerked a thumb in the direction of Noah. "I can't have the kid here, that's what's going on. And I can't have Libby leaving to take him home when I need her here."

Libby quickly explained that Janet had been the only person who even considered babysitting Noah, thanks to the hours Libby worked.

Lou grunted, shrugged his shoulders and

walked away as Garrett pulled his car keys from his pocket. "You don't need to leave," he told her quickly, "because I'll take him to my house. You can pick him up when you get off work." When Libby started to protest, he held up his hand. "No arguments. I'll see you when you get off work at your regular time."

She didn't even have a chance to argue before he and her son were walking to his car. It made her uncomfortable when he came to her rescue the way he just did. The more she was around Garrett, the more she wondered if leaving Desperation might be a wise idea.

"This is so cool," Noah said from the back-seat of Garrett's sports car.

"Glad you like it," Garrett replied. "Sorry it's so cramped."

"Oh, it isn't," Noah said, his voice filled with awe.

Garrett was barely listening. He hadn't imagined how difficult Libby's life must be, juggling all that she did. He wasn't about to let her lose her job, and if that meant not allowing her to turn down his offer to help, so be it.

It didn't bother him that he wasn't spending time at Lou's, although he had been a bit stir-crazy when Paige had offered to take care of

Sophie for the evening. But that had passed when he walked into Lou's and saw Libby. Even more so, now that he had something positive to do.

Noah broke into his thoughts, asking about Sophie.

"She's good," Garrett answered, remembering the hug she'd given him when he left for Lou's. She might not have spoken, but she knew exactly how to melt his heart. If it hadn't been for his sister's insistence that he go out, he'd have stayed home with his daughter.

As he pulled into his driveway, Garrett realized that his offer to take Noah home with him might turn out to be an even better idea than he'd imagined. Noah would be great company for Sophie.

But when he opened the front door and stepped inside, he discovered that Sophie was sound asleep in bed. Even Noah looked disappointed as Garrett chatted with Paige and Tucker, and then thanked them as they left.

The rest of the evening wasn't a waste, though, and he enjoyed the time with Noah as they shared soft drinks and watched a late season baseball game on TV. By the time Libby arrived to pick up her son, Garrett had been formulating an idea that might work well for both him and Libby.

"I've been thinking," he said, after Libby had passed on a soft drink, iced tea and a glass of water.

"So have I," she said, before he could continue. "Maybe Noah and I should move to Oklahoma City or Tulsa."

Garrett instantly noted that she appeared to be unable to look him in the eye. Neither did she seem to be enjoying her idea. He didn't blame her. In spite of the usual negatives of small towns, Desperation was a good place to live and raise a child. Even he'd figured that out.

"That's the worst idea I've heard in a long time," he told her, determined to keep her from leaving when she didn't need to.

For the briefest moment, before she ducked her head, he thought he saw the glimmer of tears in her eyes. His heart ached with the need to help her. "It isn't easy, is it?" he asked softly.

She lifted her head and sighed. "No, it isn't."

But Garrett wasn't going to give up. Not yet. He glanced at Noah, who seemed to be involved in what was on television, before turning his attention fully to Libby. "You asked me earlier how I was. To be honest, it hasn't been as easy as I thought it would be. I can now say I completely understand how difficult being a parent can be. Especially a single parent with a job."

Her smile was understanding. "It can be painful to learn things the hard way, but experience is the best teacher. I'm sorry you have to go through it, but it'll probably make you a better person."

"Learning from our mistakes?"

She smiled. "Always. But being a parent is never a mistake. A surprise at times, maybe, but never a mistake."

He wondered about her past, but he didn't feel comfortable asking. "I've come up empty-handed on finding someone to watch Sophie," he admitted. "We're both in the same boat, Libby."

"Along with others, I'm sure."

He didn't doubt it. "Very possible. But there isn't time to start a movement here in Desperation for more and better child care." He hoped she saw the humor in what he was saying and would at least consider the proposition he was ready to offer her. "I can't work *and* take care of Sophie, Libby, any more than you can with Noah. And neither one of us seems to be able to find someone we can trust with our kids."

"Good child care is hard to find."

Garrett nodded. He hadn't expected that his role as a father would involve all that it had already. But even though the past couple of weeks hadn't been storybook perfect, he'd continued working toward making it that way someday. He realized that not only did he have a lot to learn, but that he wouldn't give up having his daughter with him for anything.

"So here's the deal," he said, hoping what he was about to suggest wouldn't sound completely crazy. "We share child care. I work days. You work nights. We'll be comfortable that our kids are safe."

Her eyebrows shot up, arching over her amber eyes.

"Don't say no, Libby," he hurried to say, before she had a chance to turn him down without giving it some thought. "Think about it, at least, for a few days."

"I don't know…" She closed her eyes and pressed her lips together.

"Noah and I had a great evening, didn't we, Noah?" He turned to look at Noah, who had forgone watching TV and was listening intently to their conversation.

"Mom?"

Libby opened her eyes and looked at her son. "What?"

"He has a good point."

She shook her head and then turned to Garrett. "There's at least one problem. I work six nights a week."

"Six?"

"Monday through Saturday," she said, nodding. "I doubt that fits your lifestyle, but Lou needs the help, and I need the money. Raising a child doesn't come cheap."

The financial aspect wasn't something Garrett had even given a thought to, not when it came to himself. Money—or more precisely the lack of it—had never been a problem for him. "You could save money by not having to pay for babysitting," he pointed out, hoping it would sway her to accept.

"But what about your time? I mean, you have a life and—"

"To tell the truth, I don't have much of a social life. You can ask my sister. So there's no problem there."

"What about those times when you might have to leave town?" she asked. "I mean, I've heard you sometimes go into Oklahoma City on city business."

He didn't have a ready answer, but that

didn't stop him. "We'll work something out. It doesn't happen all that often."

He could tell he was gaining ground when she glanced again at Noah, but he knew he hadn't convinced her yet. What else could he say that would win her over to his idea?

Seconds ticked by before she let out a long sigh. "I suppose we could try it. For a little while, anyway. If it doesn't work out—"

"Then I'll find us both child care somewhere else."

She hesitated and then nodded. "I guess that's fair."

It was. He knew it was. And he was convinced that it wasn't just the only answer, but the perfect one. As long as he kept things on a friendly basis and nothing more, everything would be fine.

"Mom, I'm home!"

Libby looked up from the laundry she was sorting, just as Noah closed the front door behind him. "I see that. How was football practice?"

"Good." Tossing his book bag to the sofa, he hurried to the corner of the room where Sophie was playing with a small dollhouse Garrett had bought to keep at Libby's. When

Noah sat down next to her, she turned to look at him and smiled, then nodded to the tiny family that had come with the dollhouse.

He picked up the small father figure that lay off to the side. "It's almost time for the dad to come home from work," he told Sophie. "He's probably hungry, and so am I."

She giggled and picked up one of the other dolls, but she said nothing.

Sighing, Libby wondered how long it would take the little girl to be comfortable enough to speak. She knew Garrett worried even more about Sophie's silence, and Libby had tried her best to ease his fears, even as her own began to grow. All she could do was hope and pray that in time Sophie would understand that no one was going to leave her or send her away.

Libby set aside the laundry and walked to the small kitchen. "There's a few doughnuts left from the ones Garrett brought this morning," she called to the children. "Anybody want one?"

"I do!" Noah shouted.

"Wash your hands first," Libby reminded him. "And take your backpack to your room."

Minutes later, Noah and Sophie pulled out chairs and settled at the table. "Sophie washed her hands, too," Noah told his mother.

Placing a paper plate with a doughnut in front of Sophie, Libby smiled. "Good for you!"

Sophie returned the smile and nodded, her eyes sparkling, and then she attacked her doughnut.

Kids will be kids, Libby thought, silently laughing to herself. Sitting at the table with them, she took a bite of her own doughnut. Garrett had brought them for breakfast, but pastries weren't her idea of a nutritious meal. She even tried to stay away from sugary cereals. But now that they were sharing child care, Garrett had brought something every morning that week for breakfast or for snacks. She appreciated his gesture and had decided not to mention her concerns. Yet. None of which meant she wasn't enjoying the goodies he brought.

He had a lot to learn about being a parent. She didn't doubt he knew that. In fact, doubting himself when it came to his parenting skills was probably his biggest fault. He needed to have more faith in himself. He was doing much better than many men she'd known.

Her ex-husband's face popped into her mind. He was one man who hadn't had a clue about being a father, and he didn't care that he didn't. But that was the past, she reminded herself quickly and shoved the thought of him from her mind.

After finishing her doughnut, she reminded Noah and Sophie to wash the sticky from their hands when they finished. Of course the reminder brought a groan from her son. She ignored it. He was a good kid but also a normal one, therefore he was far from perfect. She understood and accepted that, and didn't want it any other way.

"Can we watch TV?" he asked after the two of them had cleaned up again.

Libby glanced at the clock. It was getting close to time for Garrett to pick up Sophie, which also meant it was time to start getting ready for work. "Sure, but keep the volume down, okay?"

Thirty minutes later, she was changed and almost ready to leave, but Garrett still hadn't arrived. The fact that he was late had her worried. The last she'd heard, he planned to take Sophie and Noah to the Chick-a-Lick Café for their supper. He was usually punctual, so they'd made no contingency plans if he was held up at the office.

When she heard a light knock on the door, she was relieved to find Garrett on the other side. There was enough to worry about besides him being late, and she decided that they needed to at least talk about a backup plan for the future. He might not want to think about it, but anything could happen to upset their schedule.

As he walked to the dollhouse where Sophie was playing, Libby wasn't sure how to let him know that she was upset. Experience had taught her that everything that went wrong was her fault. She'd thought that she'd finally convinced herself that wasn't true, but the lesson had obviously ingrained itself in her.

She looked at her watch. If she didn't leave in the next ten minutes, she'd be late for her shift. Lou expected his employees to be prompt.

"I'm late, aren't I?" Garrett asked.

Her head snapped up and she stared at him. "Well, um, just a little," she answered, her old fear returning. "But it's okay," she hurried to tell him. She knew she shouldn't be reacting this way, but she couldn't stop.

He glanced at his watch, too, and sighed. "You'd better get going, hadn't you? I promise this won't happen again."

Out of habit that even time hadn't broken, her body stiffened at the words he'd just spoken, and she waited for something to happen.

Clasping her hands tightly in front of her, all she could do was nod. "It's—it's all right."

It didn't help when Garrett stood watching her, studying her, as if he could see inside her head and know everything.

"Go on to work," he said, taking her by surprise. "We'll lock up." He looked around the room. "Is there anything else I should do?"

Somehow she regained some control of herself and was able to move toward the door. "No, everything is good. Just lock the door and turn off all the lights except that lamp in the corner. Noah knows." She smiled at her son and hated that she'd reverted to her old ways. "I'll pick you up later, honey, and you be good for Garrett, okay?"

He hurried to her as she opened the door and slipped his arms around her waist, hugging her. When she looked down at him, he was looking up at her. "It's okay, Mom. I can take care of it."

Tears stung her eyes, and all she could do was nod. Running her fingers through his dark, curly hair, she did her best to smile, and then slipped out the door.

A busy night at the tavern usually kept her mind off her troubles, but Libby discovered it didn't always work. While she took orders, served beer, wiped tables and walked what seemed like miles, she couldn't stop thinking of how she'd slipped back into her past behavior. By the time work ended for the night, she was certain Garrett had noticed that something was wrong with her and would call off their child care agreement when she picked up Noah.

With her pockets full of tip change after a night that was at least productive in the world of work, she stood on the broad porch of Garrett's home and listened to the quiet drone of the TV inside. She felt badly because Garrett was getting the worst part of their deal. While she only watched over Sophie on Monday through Friday, Garrett had to curtail his social life on Saturdays to keep an eye on Noah. If she wasn't so tired and worried, she'd remind him that the child care they shared should be divided more equally.

Lifting her hand, she rapped on the door and within seconds it opened. A golden glow from a lamp lit the inside of the house and welcomed her. She stepped inside and Garrett closed the door behind her.

"You look tired," he said.

"Only a little," she answered, not wanting to admit it. Moving farther into the room, she noticed that Noah wasn't present and must be sleeping. She hated to have to wake him to drive home, but he never complained. That was how it had been for the past eight months since they'd moved to Desperation, and they'd both adjusted to it.

The large, comfortable sofa tempted her to sit and relax, but she ignored the lure, knowing she might not get up again until morning. Instead, she gathered the courage she'd fought for and won six years ago when she divorced her abusive husband. She and Garrett needed to discuss a backup plan in case either of them discovered they would be late or had to have a day off.

She turned to Garrett and reminded herself that she was no longer a woman who wasn't allowed to speak her mind. "I wanted you to know that I was worried today that you were going to be late."

He nodded, his expression solemn. "I know, and I'm sorry I made you worry."

She tried not to focus on how easy it was for him to say it. His sincerity seemed natural and surprised her. "It's all right," she managed to say. "I'm only thinking of the future. We need to come up with a backup plan, just in case. There must be someone we could call in a pinch, but I don't know of anyone."

Garrett perched on the arm of the sofa. "I'm the one who is more likely to be late. Or there's always that possibility that I'd have to be gone, although I want to keep that at a minimum for Sophie's sake. Let me see if I can find someone who could take over at the last minute."

Libby was relieved she didn't have to handle this alone. "All right. I won't worry about it unless I have to." She knew this was her chance to bring up the imbalance of time they each had the children, but she decided not to, until they had the other solved. "Noah's asleep?" she asked.

"About nine-thirty," Garrett answered. "And we did homework as soon as we got home from the café. You do know how smart he is, don't you?"

She laughed. "I guess I'm so accustomed to it, I take it for granted. Thank you for helping him with the homework. He'll try to skip doing it if he thinks he can."

"Most kids do," Garrett said, getting to his feet.

She forced herself to move. "I'd better get him home."

He followed her as she walked down the

hallway to his bedroom, where Noah slept on the bed, covered with a blanket. "Noah," she whispered. "It's time to go home."

The boy slowly opened his eyes and sat up, reaching for his jacket beside him. "Okay," he mumbled.

When they reached the front door, Garrett stopped her. "I'll find someone to help out when needed."

She didn't doubt that he would at least try, and she thanked him. In the quiet of her car, with Noah tucked into the backseat, she wondered again if the agreement she and Garrett had made to share child care had been a good idea. To her surprise and pleasure, it was working well, especially now that she felt assured that they would have a backup person. She no longer had to worry about losing her child care and, to top it off, she enjoyed having Sophie around.

But she did worry that she was getting too close to Garrett. She knew better than to trust anyone, but he had been so helpful, it was tempting to simply take her problems to him. She couldn't do that, though, and she would have to be more careful to keep her emotions out of the arrangement. But that wasn't proving to be as easy as she'd hoped it would be.

Chapter Five

Garrett felt a tug on his rolled-up shirtsleeve and looked down to see Sophie. Tired and grumpy from a long, exhausting day dealing with the city council, he nearly snapped at her, but managed to bite back words he had no business saying. After taking a deep breath and letting it out, he felt a ton of sympathy for working mothers.

"What is it, Sophie?" he asked, as if she would actually answer. Just one more thing to add to his growing list of exasperations.

She smiled, ducked her head and then pointed to the table.

He couldn't be angry with her for not speaking. It wasn't as if she seemed to be blaming him for this latest upheaval in her life. Besides, even in her silence, she was a ray of sunshine, no matter how tired he was.

"Yes, you can set the table, Sophie," he answered, aware that they were running behind.

They'd fallen into a routine, Noah included, and she obviously didn't want it interrupted… or delayed, as was happening tonight.

"Chow time," he announced. He pulled out his own chair while the children did the same. Watching Sophie climb on top of a stack of old law books to boost her high enough to reach the table, he thought of all the other families that were repeating the ritual. It came without warning and surprised him. He loved his own family—his parents and sister—but he'd never seriously considered having a family of his own.

"How was football practice?" he asked Noah.

Noah looked up. "Okay."

"What position do you play?"

"All of 'em," Noah answered.

Garrett considered it and decided that was fair. Playing all positions gave everyone a chance to understand each one and learn where their strengths were, before going on to competition in school when they were a little older.

"Did you know Sophie can be a cheerleader next year?" Noah asked.

"Really? Isn't that kind of young? Who chooses them?"

"Oh, nobody chooses them. All you have to do is pay, and she's a cheerleader."

Garrett looked at his daughter, who was watching him closely. He couldn't tell what she was thinking. Was that something she might like to do? He could imagine her on the field, pom-poms waving wildly as she cheered for the team on the field, and he smiled.

And then reality struck. Until she decided to talk, he shouldn't even dream of making plans. And then there was school. She should probably be in pre-kindergarten, at least according to Paige, but he didn't know if she'd been attending school anywhere and had no way to find out. He didn't even know where to start and hoped he could remember to ask Libby if she had any ideas about what he should do.

When dinner was over, Noah and Sophie watched television, while Garrett loaded the dishwasher and straightened the kitchen. Something had come over him, and he couldn't put his finger on what was bothering him. He missed sharing evenings with his sister and realized his only social life had been to stop in at Lou's a few times a week for a cup of coffee, or the occasional visit to the Rocking O Ranch to visit with Jules and Tanner O'Brien and their friends. *His* friends. But there was something else, and he didn't know what it was he was missing.

It wasn't long before Sophie was yawning, and he scooped her into his arms and took her to her bedroom. Paige had given her a book of fairy tales, and once he had Sophie tucked into bed, she pointed to the book on the shelf.

"Which story?" He took the book and settled on the bed next to her so she could see the pictures as he read.

She turned the pages, until she came to the story of Rapunzel. He'd only read two pages before she was sound asleep next to him.

He found Noah at the table doing homework and asked if the boy needed help. Noah shook his head. "Thanks, but math is easy."

Garrett had noticed Noah's good manners the first time they met. Had that been only a few weeks ago? So much had happened, it was hard to believe. Three weeks ago, he'd been a typical single man, thirty-four years old, with an excellent career he enjoyed in a small town in Oklahoma he'd grown to love. Now he was the single dad of a four-year-old daughter, spending his evenings and half of his weekends with two children under the age of ten. Even he was amazed.

Grabbing his briefcase, he spread the files from work he needed to study on the coffee table. The house was quiet and as he read, his eyelids grew heavy. He heard a woman's sultry voice call his name, and he smiled as he looked around and found her. The blonde was a dead ringer for Libby, but it couldn't be. Not in that red dress and those bedroom eyes. He reached out, intending to pull her closer and settle her on his lap. That's all it would take—

"What do you think you're doing?"

The voice wasn't loud, but it had lost the sultry sound, causing him to frown. "What does it look like?" he asked, wishing she'd just give in and enjoy the moment.

"Garrett, wake up!"

Wake up? He tried, but it was like swimming up from the bottom of a deep pool, and as he forced his eyes open, Libby's face slowly came into focus. He felt her tug and realized that he was holding her hand, keeping her from moving away. "Sorry," he mumbled, as he let go, then ran his hand down his face. "I must have—"

"Fallen asleep?" she finished, quickly stepping back, now that she was free.

He sat up straight, wishing his mind would clear, and saw the pile of papers on the table in front of him. Noah, he noticed, was curled up on a nearby chair, sound asleep. "I was working and, yeah, must've fallen asleep."

"Worn out by a couple of kids," she said and shook her head. "Isn't that kind of pitiful?" But the hint of a smile was proof she was teasing. Before he could think of a fitting reply, she asked, "By the way, where's Sophie?"

"In bed. She fell asleep while I was reading to her. You look pretty tired, too."

"At least I didn't fall asleep while I was working."

"You've got me there."

Neither of them said anything for several moments, until Garrett finally broke the moment. "When was the last time you went out and did something different?"

Her expression shifted. "Different than what?"

He noticed she'd chosen her words carefully and knew he would need to do the same. He'd discovered that there seemed to be two Libbys. One was the Libby at Lou's, who flirted and smiled and seemed at ease with him. And then there was this one, guarded and wary. He had also become aware that the little teasing she did was often used as a defense of some kind, although he hadn't figured out why.

He answered her question carefully. "Different than what you do every day. Different than spending your day off cleaning and doing laundry."

"Ah, you know about my secret life, then."

"Yes, Mata Hari," he answered, standing and straightening what he knew was a rumpled shirt. "I've been watching you closely."

He smiled slowly as he took a step toward her. She took a small step back. Not enough that she appeared to be afraid of him, but enough to make the space he'd narrowed wider again. This, he decided, was not the time to play games, nor was it the time to try to find out more about her and what her life had been like before Desperation.

"Will you give me a hand with Noah?" she asked, breaking the moment.

"Sure."

But as he picked up Noah's backpack and helped her with the boy's jacket, he decided it was time that both he and Libby had some fun.

"But I'm a mess!" Libby looked down at her oldest pair of blue jeans and the too-small shirt that pulled at the buttons. It was Sunday, her one day off, and the day she got herself and Noah ready for the coming week, including catching up on laundry and cleaning.

"You look great," Garrett answered. "If you feel like you need to change, we have a few minutes."

A few minutes weren't going to do the trick. "I'll need to take a shower."

He propped one foot on the opposite knee and leaned back against the worn sofa. "Okay. I can wait."

Libby was tempted to tell him—beg him— to go on to the Rocking O Ranch without her. He'd sprung this little visit, which included a barbecue and time with his friends—people she barely knew and rarely spoke with—at the last minute by knocking on her door not five minutes ago and telling her they were all going. He obviously knew that she would have declined the invitation if Noah hadn't been so eager to go.

Garrett was as cool as a cucumber and totally certain of himself. Once upon a time, she'd been much the same way. Life had changed her, and she'd be lying if she said she didn't miss the long ago past, before she'd met Eric Cabrera and everything had changed, including her.

Garrett wasn't going to let her get out of this, so all she could do was agree and hope she didn't embarrass anyone. "All right," she told him. The corners of his mouth turned up only the slightest, but she didn't miss it and let out an exasperated sigh. "But only because Noah has been begging to visit his friend Kirby."

"Whatever it takes," Garrett replied, without bothering to glance at her.

She worried about what to wear as she showered and washed her hair. Garrett had insisted the monthly barbecue was casual. Jeans or whatever she felt comfortable wearing was fine. No one would be in tuxes or evening gowns, he'd assured her. Good thing, she thought, because she'd left her evening gowns and the fur wrap behind when she'd packed her car to the top of the roof and lit out of Phoenix with Noah, praying Eric wouldn't find them and take Noah from her permanently.

Twenty minutes later, dressed in clean jeans, a lightweight blue sweater and a pair of leather slides she'd forgotten she had, she walked into her tiny living room and cleared her throat.

Garrett, still on the sofa, turned to look and gave a long, low whistle. "Wow, you look great, Libby," he said, as he got to his feet.

Noah, who'd joined Garrett on the sofa while she was getting ready, gave his opinion, too. "You're the prettiest mom of all."

Libby's hands were cold and she rubbed them together, hoping her smile hid her nervousness. "Well, if everyone's ready…"

Sophie, who'd been silently playing with the dollhouse in the corner, raced to Libby and grabbed her hand. Looking up at Libby, she smiled and nodded, then tugged her toward the door.

"Has Sophie met Jules?" Libby asked, as they drove the few miles to the O'Briens' ranch.

"Not yet," Garrett answered, turning the car onto a graveled drive, lined with trees. "Jules has been at a seminar, and then had to testify at an appropriations hearing, so this is the first chance there's been to visit her."

He glanced at Libby, and she noticed he was gripping the steering wheel so tight, his knuckles were white. "It'll be fine," she assured him, keeping her voice as quiet as possible.

He didn't speak until he'd brought the car to a stop in front of a two-story white house, complete with a wide porch that wrapped around the front and along the length of one side. "Whatever Jules says, it's better than being in the dark. I just hope she can shed a little light on it, that's all."

Without thinking, Libby put her hand on his as he continued to grip the steering wheel, and she gave it an encouraging squeeze. When he turned his hand and captured hers in it to return the squeeze, she felt things she didn't remember ever feeling. She had to force herself to breathe and then to gently pull her hand away.

The moment was thankfully broken when she and Garrett exited the car and helped Noah and Sophie from the backseat. She wondered if she would be able to eat a bite of food. Whether from being nervous about meeting the O'Briens and Garrett's other friends or from what she'd felt when he'd held her hand, she didn't trust herself or her stomach. But she was here, and she'd make the best of the evening, no matter what.

"We're around back!" someone shouted.

"Sounds like Tanner," Garrett said. "You know him and Jules, right?"

"We've met." And that was about all, Libby thought. Oh, she'd seen them at Lou's, even waited on them a few times. And she'd encountered them in town, here and there. They'd said hello or nodded in greeting, but they didn't know each other well enough to stop and chat. They were acquaintances and nothing more. She didn't expect this visit to change things.

Garrett led them toward the back of the house, and even before they reached it, she could hear the laughter of adults and children. They were nice people, she was sure, and she might have been at ease if things were different.

"We made it," he announced as they rounded the corner of the house.

There was an end-of-September chill in the air, and Libby was glad she'd slipped on a light jacket. She'd expected there to be fewer people. She counted at least four couples and several children of varying ages, from barely toddling to teens, gathered on a patio lit by strings of tiny lights and a few scattered torches.

As Noah hurried off to join the children, Libby quickly reminded herself that this wasn't all that different than seeing these people at Lou's or at various places in Desperation. But knowing that didn't necessarily put her at ease. She was on their turf now, although she definitely appreciated Jules O'Brien's friendly smile.

"Libby! I'm so glad you're here." Jules hurried over and took her hand. "Garrett said he might be bringing someone, but he wouldn't tell us who." She slid a look at Garrett with a twinkle in her eye. "Thank you for coming, both of you."

Libby wondered why Garrett hadn't mentioned who he might be bringing, but decided it wasn't important. She watched as Jules knelt down in front of Sophie and introduced herself. Sophie hung back at first, but in seconds she was smiling and nodding.

Jules spoke quietly to Sophie and then to Garrett, before taking the little girl into the house. Libby mentally crossed her fingers that Jules would either be able to get Sophie to talk or, at the very least, could give them news that there was truly nothing really wrong. She knew Garrett was greatly concerned about why Sophie was choosing not to speak.

Just as Dusty McPherson, Tanner O'Brien's friend and business partner, walked up to talk to Garrett, Libby heard someone hail her from the other side of the large patio. She turned to see Dusty's wife waving her over. Kate was famous for her cooking, and it was her barbecue sandwiches that were served at Lou's, so Libby knew her better than she knew the others, although they weren't what most people would call friends. Wearing what she hoped was a friendly and relaxed smile, she approached Kate.

"It's good to see you," Kate greeted her. "We don't get the chance very often. You're always busy when I stop by Lou's, and I don't want to get him mad at either of us."

Libby laughed. Kate knew Lou almost as well as she did. "Lou needs those sandwiches," she said, "so you're safe. And I usually only have Sundays off, so there isn't a lot of time for socializing."

"Summers are like that for me," Kate answered, nodding, "at least when it comes to farming. Fall, too, but not as much."

"And then there's your pies and cakes and your catering."

Kate leaned closer. "Catering was Dusty's idea, but I have to admit I enjoy it. Most of the time. Don't tell him I said so, though." When the shriek of what sounded like a child was heard, she spun around. "Be right back," she said over her shoulder as she hurried away.

Libby watched as Kate gathered her twin boys and led them away from the patio and onto the grass. After getting down on their level, she appeared to be speaking to each one, glancing now and then to a blond-haired angel of a little girl who had to belong to Kate's sister, Trish, who stood watching the whole thing. The three small children shared a birthday and were just over a year old. Even so, mischief glowed in the eyes of the two little boys.

Dusty marched over to the four of them and immediately scooped each of the boys into a football hold, one under each arm, and grinned at his wife. Even at a distance, Libby could see the love the two of them shared.

"They don't have a clue what I said to them," Kate told Libby, laughing, when she returned. "And they seem to be at their orneriest tonight. At least they can't really run yet. When that happens, I don't know what I'll do. Hand them over to their daddy to finish raising, I guess."

Libby laughed. "I can barely remember when Noah was that age. He was a good baby, but a curious one, once he discovered crawling. And when he started walking? Look out, world."

They talked more about the perils of raising children, and Trish joined them, greeting Libby with the same kindness Kate and Jules had. Libby was amazed at how wonderful she felt, just talking to other women who were her age. Even after she'd divorced Eric, she'd kept socializing to a minimum. He was the son of wealthy parents with connections, in addition to having his own. Anything she did was bound to get back to him, and she didn't dare do anything that might anger him, even when they were no longer married.

She'd begun to relax and enjoy herself, when Jules returned with Sophie. The concern on Garrett's face nearly broke her heart, and she watched as Jules and Sophie joined him. Within seconds, Jules looked up and waved her over to them.

"Since you're Sophie's caregiver, you should know what I've determined," Jules told her. Leaning down to Sophie, she whispered in her ear and the little girl skipped across the patio to where Noah was playing with his friend Kirby.

"Is she all right?" Garrett asked immediately.

Jules's smile was comforting. "If you mean is Sophie's silence permanent, my professional guess is that it isn't. You did say that Paige checked her out thoroughly and found no damage to her hearing, right?"

Garrett nodded. "She can hear, plain as day. She just won't talk."

"She giggles and laughs," Libby added, "especially when she's playing with Noah. And I've heard her humming, too."

Jules turned to look directly at Garrett. "You have no idea of what her life was like before her mother sent her to you? Where they lived? If anyone lived with them?"

Garrett shook his head as he lowered it. "None at all. I walked into my office and there she was, with a short letter from her mother, telling me Sophie was my daughter and she was giving her to me to raise."

"It was a shock, I'm sure, and I know you're worried. I would be, too, in the same situation. Is there anyone you can get in touch with who might know something? About her mother, at least."

"Maybe Sophie's grandmother," he answered. "But I can't even be sure of that. I only met her once, and that was by accident. She and Sophie's mother weren't close."

"Do what you can," Jules encouraged him. "All I can tell you is that she simply isn't ready to speak yet."

"But you think she will?" he asked, a hopeful note in his voice.

"I'm positive she's choosing not to talk. I don't know why, but it could be a trust issue. Maybe when she feels she can trust you or Libby she'll speak. I suspect it'll happen when you—and Sophie—least expect it, so don't be surprised when it does—or doesn't happen."

"I'm sure you're right," Garrett told her, then turned to Libby. "I guess we'll just go on as we have been."

With nothing else she could do to help, Libby offered him an encouraging smile. "We'll give it time," she said, and turned to Jules. "Thank you."

Jules pressed a hand to Garrett's arm and the other hand to Libby's. "Anytime. I'm always here, if either of you need me."

For a brief second, Libby was tempted to speak privately with Jules about her past, but the moment was gone in a breath. Sharing any of what had happened that led her to Desperation could too easily be a mistake. Her past would have to remain a secret.

Garrett didn't feel a whole lot better after talking with Jules, but he swore he would stop worrying so much and let Sophie choose her time to speak. In the meantime, he'd remain positive that she would.

As the group of friends was called to the buffet table set up on the patio, Paige and Tucker arrived. Garrett hurried over to pull his sister aside and tell her what Jules had said.

"I'm glad you checked with Jules," Paige told him. "Just give Sophie some time. I know it's hard, but she's a healthy little girl. She needs to get to know you, that's all. Now, is that Libby I see at the table?"

"It is," he answered, leading her to the group

filling their plates. "It took some doing, but I managed to convince her to come tonight."

"Good for you. And it looks like she's having a good time."

Garrett watched as Libby laughed with Nikki MacGregor, Tanner's sister.

"Hey, Garrett."

Garrett turned to see Morgan Rule approaching. "No cuts, Sheriff," he joked. "You know that."

Morgan chuckled and gave him an easy punch on the arm. "One of the drawbacks of being a lawman, I guess. And speaking of the job, when you have a few minutes tomorrow, could you come by the office? I need to talk to you about the Skinner thing."

Garrett sobered immediately. An accident involving teen drinking had left a fifteen-year-old paralyzed, and some in the town were out for blood when it came to the driver. Neither Garrett nor Morgan wanted to see anything happen that shouldn't. "I'll stop by in the morning, if that works."

Morgan nodded. "Is that Libby Carter with my wife?"

Garrett noticed that Libby was smiling as she held Trish and Morgan's little daughter. "Yeah, and I think she's having a good time."

"Who wouldn't? There's nothing like an O'Brien barbecue for having fun." Morgan leaned closer. "You two have something going on?"

Morgan's question caused Garrett to stare at him. "Nothing. Nothing at all, except she watches Sophie during the day, while I keep an eye on her boy at night while she's at work."

"Sounds like a good arrangement. You made a good choice. She's a nice lady."

"Yeah, she is," Garrett agreed. But he wondered if everyone there was thinking there was something special going on between him and Libby. Not that he would mind, if they hadn't been parents, but they both had their hands full. Too full to carry on anything outside of child care.

He continued to assure himself into the next day that he and Libby were friends helping each other and nothing more. After spending an hour the next morning with Morgan discussing the Skinner case, Garrett decided to see if he could find Shana's parents' phone number in the book. With luck, they were still listed as living in Chicago, and he dialed the number.

Just as he was about to hang up, thinking no

one was home, he heard a hello. "Mrs. Dickinson?" he asked.

"Yes?" The voice was hesitant.

"This is Garrett Miles, Mrs. Dickinson," he said, hoping she would remember him. "Your daughter, Shana, and I saw each other for a while."

"You're Sophie's father."

The statement took him aback for a moment. "Yes, yes, I am. I wasn't sure if you knew."

"I told Shana the minute she told me she was pregnant that she should let you know. She didn't, did she?"

"No, she didn't. I only learned a few weeks ago."

"Foolish girl," she muttered.

He knew Shana and her mother didn't get along well. Shana's birth had come as a complete surprise to her older parents. He'd always suspected that when Shana had become hard to handle, her parents had thrown money at her, just so they wouldn't have to deal with her problems. But that was something he'd put together from pieces he'd heard, long after he and Shana had gone their separate ways.

"Do you know where Shana is, Mrs. Dickinson?" he asked, physically crossing the fingers on one hand. He needed all the help he could get, even if it was a bit superstitious.

Nola Dickinson snorted on the other end of line. "The last I heard—I think it was last winter—she was talking about Florida."

"Then you don't know that she's given Sophie to me," he said.

"She has, has she? Good. Sophie needs a stable life. Arthur had a stroke three years ago, and he isn't doing well. I couldn't raise Sophie, even though I knew Shana was doing a terrible job of it. From what I heard from friends—never from Shana, mind you—Sophie spent more time with babysitters and her friends than she did with her mother."

"I was afraid of that," he admitted, before he realized he'd said it.

"You'll take good care of her, I'm sure," the woman said. "You seemed like a good, stable man, and I never could understand how you got mixed up with somebody as flighty and irresponsible as my daughter."

Garrett couldn't decide if he should thank her or not. "Just one more thing, if you don't mind?"

"I need to get back to my husband, but if you'll be quick…"

"Do you know if Sophie had any... I guess you could call it speech problems?"

"Hmm, well, I did have a friend who told me that she'd heard from someone else that the last time she'd seen Shana and Sophie, oh, a few months ago, Sophie was very quiet. But that's all I know."

"But she talked before that?" he hurried to ask, before she ended the call.

"Oh, yes." She sighed. "Shana would put her on the phone, hoping I'd feel sorry and give her the money she wanted. Of course I couldn't say no to that little girl."

"Of course. And you should get back to Mr. Dickinson. Thank you for speaking with me."

"Take care of that little girl, Mr. Miles," she said. "And don't let her mother get her hands on her again, you hear?"

"I won't," he answered. At least he had a clue as to where to start looking.

Chapter Six

Libby slowly opened her eyes and stretched, then looked over at the sleeping child next to her. Dark eyelashes rested on cheeks sprinkled lightly with freckles. The hint of a smile lifted Sophie's lips as she slept. Libby couldn't believe how easy it was to take care of her and hoped Noah was half as good for Garrett.

Sitting up carefully, so as not to wake Sophie from her nap, Libby looked at the clock. Noah would be home from school soon and she needed to get something started for supper. Garrett had told her that morning when he'd dropped off Sophie that he might be later than usual picking her up. He'd talked with

Sophie's grandmother. Although he hadn't learned much, it had made him more determined to make his daughter legally his.

After running a brush through her hair, Libby went to the kitchen and began placing the cooled cookies she and Sophie had baked after lunch on a plate for Noah's after-school snack. She wasn't aware Sophie had finished her nap until she heard humming coming from the corner where the dollhouse sat. Picking up the plate of cookies, she walked into the living room and knelt next to the little girl. "Would you like a cookie? It's cool enough to eat now."

Sophie looked up and smiled, then carefully chose a cookie from the plate.

"Next time we'll decorate them," Libby said, planning ahead. "But they're good like this, aren't they?"

Sophie nodded as she munched away. Libby ate a cookie, too, as Sophie placed the family in different rooms in the dollhouse. The dolls were a family of four, with a father, mother, boy and girl. What some might think was the typical American family, Libby guessed. It was something she suspected Sophie knew nothing about. Noah's memories were probably much the same. One-parent families were becoming the norm, and it saddened her. Children deserved two parents. Two good, loving parents. Noah had once had two, but one couldn't be trusted not to hurt him.

Shaking the depressing thoughts from her mind, she stood and returned to the kitchen to start supper. It wasn't long before Noah was home, dumping his backpack on the sofa, giving his mom a hug and then joining Sophie in the corner with the dollhouse.

Libby had talked with Noah about Sophie and how she didn't speak to anyone. She'd asked if he thought the little girl was sad or missing her mother. He'd answered no, but she still wondered, and especially about what Sophie's life had been like before coming to live with Garrett. Just as they were leaving the barbecue on Sunday night, Jules had mentioned that Sophie might never talk about her life before she'd been dropped off with Garrett. She cautioned both of them not to push Sophie, but to let her take the lead when it came to when to talk and what to talk about. Libby understood, and she and Garrett had both agreed that was best, but she knew they would both wonder, nonetheless.

With nothing to do until dinner, Libby went to her bedroom and straightened the comforter, mussed during Sophie's nap, then put away a stack of clothes she'd left on a chair after doing laundry.

She was in the hallway, on her way back to the living room, when she heard Noah talking quietly to Sophie.

"It's almost time for dinner," he was saying. "Where's the mommy? And the sister?"

"Here. They're here and *hungry!*"

Libby smiled.

And then she stopped.

Had Sophie spoken?

"Me, too," Noah said.

And then Libby heard, "Is the daddy coming home?"

Libby leaned against the wall, her knees weak with relief and tears of joy in her eyes. Sophie could speak!

She could hardly wait until Garrett came to pick up his daughter. He would be so happy! The thought had her shoving away from the wall and wiping the tears from her eyes. But before she stepped out of the hall and into the living room, she stopped again, realization hitting her like a boulder.

She wasn't supposed to hear Sophie. It had been an accident that she'd overheard. If she were to tell Garrett, he would expect to hear

Sophie talk. But Libby had a bad feeling Sophie wouldn't. *When she's ready,* Jules had said.

The last thing Libby wanted to do was deceive Garrett by keeping the news from him, but she'd been deceiving him and everyone she'd met since leaving Phoenix eight months ago. Both deceptions were necessary, no matter how sad it made her feel to fool people. She was an honest person, but when it came to her past, she couldn't reveal the abuse she'd suffered, nor could she let anyone suspect that not only had she taken her son and vanished from the home they'd made after the divorce, but she'd had help and couldn't reveal from whom. And here she was again, considering adding to her list of deceptions. But a question kept running through her mind. If she told Garrett and Sophie refused to speak, he might insist. Could that make Sophie more reticent?

She was removing the casserole from the oven when Garrett tapped on the door and walked in. Watching as Sophie jumped up and ran across the room to give him a hug, Libby felt a tug at her heart. There might not have been a shout of "Daddy!" heard, but it was definitely implied. In the few weeks Sophie had lived with her father, they'd formed a fierce bond. Libby smothered a sigh. If only she could tell him what she'd heard. But it would be even better when Sophie chose to surprise him.

Libby placed the casserole on the table. "You're right on time."

Scooping Sophie into his arms, Garrett tossed her onto his shoulder. "You didn't need to do this." He nodded toward the table Noah was setting with plates and silverware.

"I know that," Libby answered, "but I wanted to. This way you won't have to worry about getting home and finding something for all of you to eat."

Garrett glanced at his watch. "Are you going to have enough time to eat? It's nearly six."

"If I hurry." She pulled out a chair and sat down.

The others joined her at the table. Noah and Garrett talked about football and guy things, while Sophie seemed to be hanging on every word. Libby didn't have time to dawdle and finished eating long before the others.

"I'll lock up tight," Garrett told her at the door as she was leaving for her shift.

"You haven't mentioned if you found where Sophie's mother might be," she reminded him.

"It looks like it may be Florida. She'd mentioned going there to her mother a couple of times, often asking for the money to do so, I'm sure." His mouth turned down in a deep frown and he shook his head. "I've hired someone to look into it, but I'm not holding my breath."

Libby nodded. He looked so worried and dejected, she wished she could say something to cheer him up. She could tell him about hearing Sophie talking to Noah, but it might do more harm than good. Instead of being overjoyed, he might feel let down, because she chose to speak to Noah first.

"Maybe you'll get lucky," she finally told him, before walking out the door to her car.

Later, when her shift was over and she was on her way home with Noah in the backseat, after picking him up at Garrett's, she wondered if she should tell her son she'd heard Sophie. She decided to keep it to herself. If, in a week or so, Sophie still hadn't spoken to Garrett, she'd talk with Noah. Until then, she'd hope for the best.

The next day, Garrett hadn't heard anything from the agency he'd hired to find Shana. In one respect, he was glad. He didn't want to deal with a woman who would be so willing to give her child to someone who was virtually a stranger to that child. On the other, his biggest fear had become that Shana would show up

on his doorstep and demand he return Sophie
to her. That was something he could never do.
He hoped she would never try to be a part of
his or his daughter's life. To insure that would
never happen, he wanted her to sign an affida-
vit, stating that she was giving up all parental
rights. Nothing less would do.

As Libby drove away after picking up Noah
for the night, Garrett berated himself for forgetting again to ask her about school for Sophie. Shaking his head, he started to turn back
inside the house when he noticed the night sky
above. He stopped and took a deep breath, the
cool autumn air clearing his lungs and refresh-
ing his mind.

He'd always enjoyed the outdoors. He wasn't
a hunter, although when he was a boy, some
of his father's friends had been. Instead, he'd
stuck to other outdoor sports. Baseball and
swimming in the spring and summer, then
football, basketball and some hockey in the
winter kept him busy year round. He'd played
on his college baseball team, but quit when he
and his father disagreed over his decision to
become a lawyer instead of a doctor.

It had been the lure of the small town setting, surrounded by the great outdoors, that
had brought him to Desperation four years

ago. The irony was that he'd not yet taken advantage of the countryside around him. He hadn't even made time to do much running, something he'd enjoyed in Chicago and later in Cincinnati, where he'd lived for a short time with Paige.

Standing on the porch, staring at the sky, he suddenly had that eerie feeling that he wasn't alone. Glancing back into the house, he saw his daughter, dressed in her long nightgown and standing only a few feet away.

"What is it, Sophie? Did you have a bad dream?"

Instead of answering, she ran to him and wrapped her arms around his legs, trapping him. Laughing, he picked her up and held her. He looked up at the sky again, the few twinkling stars he could see in the distance seeming to call to him.

"Where's your coat?" he asked Sophie. "Would you like to go look at the stars?"

When she nodded vigorously, he set her on her feet and watched as she ran to her bedroom, reappearing immediately with her coat, socks and a pair of shoes. "Smart girl!" he said, returning to the living room to help her dress for some stargazing. He grabbed a blanket from the back of the sofa, and in minutes, she was ready and buckled into her booster seat in the car.

It was a beautiful, though chilly, night as he drove out of town, away from the street and porch lights. They were surrounded by darkness lit only by the headlights, a few distant farm yard lights and the stars above. It was late enough that there was no traffic on the dirt road where he parked.

Astronomy had been one of his favorite classes in college, and as he wrapped Sophie in her blanket and placed her on the warm hood of the car, he searched for the constellations that immediately came to mind. He pointed out Ursa Major, the Big Bear, containing the Big Dipper, one of the most recognizable of all constellations.

"Then see the Little Dipper? That bright star at the tip of the handle is the North Star." He spoke as if she understood and hoped someday she would remember this moment. "If you ever get lost at night, just look for the North Star, and it'll help you find your way." He turned and pointed to the east. "There's Gemini and Taurus, and those stars in a line are Orion's Belt."

Sophie said nothing, but he hadn't expected she would. He was enjoying sharing something that had meant a lot to him when he was younger. Maybe someday she would remember and discover her own interest in the sky.

She pointed to the Milky Way, and he explained what he knew about it. There was a lot he didn't remember, but he doubted she noticed or cared.

"Are you cold?" he asked, pulling her closer to him as they leaned back against the windshield. If anyone else had dared to sit on his car, he'd have done them bodily harm. For the little girl he'd met only a month ago, he'd do anything.

He wasn't sure when she fell asleep, but it was sometime after his arm had lost all feeling from keeping it around her. Easing her away enough to get a good hold on her, he moved her off the hood and into the car. As he drove home, he wondered what Libby would say when he told her about his night of stargazing with Sophie, and he suddenly realized he wouldn't tell her.

Libby was popping into his mind too often. He was relying on her more than he'd planned to. He'd never expected they'd see so much of each other. But he couldn't have allowed her to lose her job, and he didn't regret suggesting they share child care, not one bit.

She wasn't the Libby he knew from Lou's. Not the sassy, flirty Libby. He'd recognized that the moment she stepped into his office the day Sophie arrived. She was different then and different now.

It wasn't a bad different, just...different.

Was it because of him? He couldn't imagine why.

He'd hoped that taking her to the O'Briens' and just being with a group of people would bring back that lively Libby. It hadn't. And it didn't really matter. He was still attracted to her, maybe even more. He wasn't sure what to think. There'd been only one visit to Lou's since they'd started sharing child care, and he couldn't say that he missed it all that much. Maybe if he was honest, a lot of the reason he'd gone there was because of Libby.

Now that he understood a little of what her life was like, working nights at a tavern and raising a young son, he admired her even more.

And Sophie adored her, had from the very beginning. He owed Libby a lot.

But just how much should he allow himself to feel the things he was feeling for her? They weren't simple feelings. They weren't feelings he'd had for anyone before.

Pulling his car into the driveway, he shut off

the lights and turned off the engine. A strange sensation came over him, and he admitted to himself that he was falling for Libby. He couldn't do that. In addition to her being a single mom, now he was a single dad and he had no business having a relationship with anyone. He knew she'd understand if he told her, but he didn't believe it was right to do that. Instead, he'd just have to make sure that they kept their focus on their kids, not on each other.

He felt better, now that he'd faced his feelings for Libby and had some kind of plan about how to deal with them. As he carried Sophie into the house and to her bed, he was almost tempted to let whatever this thing with Libby was play itself out. But doing so might lead to things he'd never considered, and he wasn't a man who jumped into anything without being fully knowledgeable.

"Let's face it," he whispered to his sleeping daughter when he'd tucked her into bed, "I don't know anything about love."

"Garrett, join us," Morgan called out when Garrett stepped inside the Chick-a-Lick Café for lunch.

Garrett smiled and nodded to several other people in the café as he made his way to the booth where the sheriff and Tucker were sitting. "It's busy today," he said, looking around, as he slid into the booth next to Tucker.

"This time of day, it always is," Morgan replied.

"I'd rather come in the late morning," Tucker said, "when there aren't so many people and just enjoy the coffee. Sometimes even the company."

Before he could comment, the café door flew open, the metal bell on top clanging loudly.

"Sheriff, you need to arrest Agatha Clayborne," Letha Atkins announced as she breezed inside.

Morgan rolled his eyes before turning to the woman, who had stomped her way to their booth. "Now, Letha—"

"Don't 'now Letha' me, Morgan Rule," she announced so the whole café could hear. "I want something done, and done right now."

Morgan glanced around the room with an assuring smile, nodding to the café patrons. "What is it that I'm to arrest Aunt Aggie for doing, Letha?" he asked, his voice lowered.

Letha harrumphed. "She's parked that old truck in two parking spaces out there." She pointed to Aggie's pickup truck, parked in front of the café. "I couldn't get my car door open and had to *scoot* to the passenger side of my car to get out."

Garrett had to cover the smile on his face with his hand, as he imagined Letha, who was not a small woman, scooting across the bucket seats of her car. If nothing else, the people of Desperation were always entertaining.

"Just because she's your wife's aunt," Letha continued, "doesn't mean she's above the law. I want her arrested. This minute!"

"Simmer down, Letha," Morgan said quietly.

Letha's chin went up as she looked down her nose at all three men. "Then I'll take this up with the mayor."

"Be my guest," Morgan answered, totally unconcerned. "I heard what he told you the last time. But I will go out there right now and make sure Aggie's truck is within the white parking lines. If it isn't, I'll issue a parking ticket. *That's* what I can do."

Both Tucker and Garrett were quiet as Morgan pushed from the booth and strode through the café and out the door to Aggie's pickup. Tucker let out a loud sigh and shook his head. "I don't know what has Letha in an uproar, but she's been on the warpath for months. Usually it's Hettie that Letha's making a fuss about, but now it's spread to Aggie, and neither woman deserves it."

"Women are a strange lot," Garrett said, thinking of the change in Libby.

As if thinking of her had made her appear, Libby walked into the café with Sophie. Instead of looking for a place to sit, she stepped up to the cash register and waited.

"There's no question that little girl is yours," Tucker said.

Garrett turned to look at him. "Do you think so?"

"Yeah. But then I don't know her mama, so I notice the things I see that are like you. The only difference is that she looks like an angel. You? Not so much."

Garrett laughed at the friendly dig and watched as Libby took a paper sack from Darla, then pointed to the jar of stick candy that was always on the counter at the register. Once again, he was struck by her kindness and the way she cared for his daughter as if she were hers.

Morgan walked in, his hat pulled low over his eyes, and headed straight for the booth. "Some people," he muttered.

"What happened?" Tucker asked, as Morgan slid onto the seat across from them.

"I gave Aggie a ticket," he answered, keeping his voice low, "but I'm going to tell her to tear it up. I'll admit she was parked a bit close to the white line of that space, but she wasn't *over* the line. I think Letha Atkins pulled in as close as possible, just so she'd have something to complain about."

"Some people are like that," Garrett said.

Before they could say anything else, Darla arrived at their table to take their orders, and the talk then changed to other things, Letha Atkins not among them. Garrett enjoyed his lunch, aware that good company could always make the best of any situation.

Later that day, when he picked up Noah and Sophie to take to his house so Libby could go to work, he mentioned that he'd seen her in the café.

"You did?" she asked, a note of surprise in her voice as she scrambled to help Noah find his coat. "It was a last-minute decision when I saw that the weather might get colder tonight, so we picked up some sandwiches at the café to make it special and had a picnic in the park."

"And I missed it?" Noah asked, obviously disappointed.

"Next time," she told him and handed him his coat. Turning to Garrett, she said, "I hope

I'll be off a little earlier tonight, since I worked a little later last night. No promises, though."

"Sounds fair," he answered. "We'll look for you when we see you."

When she'd told them goodbye and was gone, he and Noah locked up the apartment, and then he drove the three of them to his house. Once they were inside, Noah shared his latest school news, while Sophie listened with what seemed to be awe. Garrett wasn't sure if it was Noah or simply talk of school, but she hung on every word.

Noah asked Garrett if he knew how to play checkers. "Sure," Garrett answered. "Do you know how?"

Noah nodded. "But I don't play often. Nobody else seems to like to play." He glanced at Sophie, who was listening, but was silent, as usual. "Do you think she's big enough to learn? I could help her. If it's okay, I mean."

"Let me see if I can find my old board," Garrett told him. In his office, he finally found the old set he'd had since he was a child, shoved into the back of a cabinet.

He returned to the living room and sat on the sofa, where he moved a few things on the coffee table, then set up the board. "Do you want red or black?" he asked Sophie, spreading the chips on the table. She pointed to the red ones, and he helped her move them to her side of the table. "Now you put them on the board. We'll use the black squares for this game, so you put all of your red checkers on the black squares on your side, and I'll put my black checkers on my side. Can you do that?"

When Noah offered to help her, she shook her head and placed her checkers correctly on the board. When she was done, she smiled proudly at Noah.

"Noah's going to help with the rest, okay?" Garrett asked her.

She looked at Noah and nodded. When she scooted over to give him more room, he reached for one of the red checkers. She put her hand on his and shook her head.

Noah released the checker, looked at Garrett and grinned. "I think she wants to do this herself."

"It's okay, honey," Garrett told her. "Noah is just going to show you how to jump and which direction you can go."

As he and Noah moved the checkers around the board, he explained slowly and carefully what she could do and what she couldn't. When they were done with the demonstration, he asked if she was ready.

She nodded, bouncing up and down, an eager light in her eyes.

"She's good," Noah said, fifteen minutes later.

Garrett looked at the last of his checkers on the board. "Yeah, she is. Go ahead, Sophie, take my last one, and then it's time for bed."

Her lower lip slowly slid out, and she refused to look at him. He was saved by the arrival of Libby. The wind had picked up, making the night seem colder, and she was eager to get home.

"Looks like fall is finally here," she said, while waiting for Noah to help a still-pouting Sophie put away the checker set.

Garrett stood with her near the door, without offering to take her coat. There was a brief in his office he needed to go over after Sophie was asleep, so unless Libby had something important to talk about, he didn't intend to keep her. "It'll warm up again," he said. "You'll see."

"It's colder than I'd thought it would be. I came from a warmer climate."

"Phoenix, wasn't it?"

She looked everywhere but at him. "Tucson."

"Definitely different weather there than we have here."

"And you're accustomed to even colder."

He noticed that Noah was now putting on his jacket. "Right. Chicago winters can be brutal."

She nodded, and her smile was nervous. He didn't mean to be unfriendly, but he hadn't found a middle ground yet, where he felt he was safe. Just standing near her made him extremely aware of her presence, and that was something that shouldn't be happening.

Noah joined her at the door, and Sophie moved to stand by Garrett. "Well," Libby said, reaching for the door handle, "I guess we'll see you in the morning when you bring Sophie by."

"Right," he said again. He was silent as they walked out, then called to them as they reached her car. "Drive safely."

He nearly groaned at the way it sounded, but there was nothing he could do. Until he found that middle ground, he had to be careful.

"Bedtime," he told Sophie, picking her up and taking her to her bedroom. There wasn't a sweeter sound in the world than her giggle as he tossed her to bounce on her bed. That was what he needed to focus on.

Later, as he pored over legal papers in his office, he rubbed the bridge of his nose with his thumb and forefinger. Why was it that he'd wanted to be an attorney? But he knew the answer to that. Time and again, he'd been able to help people who needed someone who understood the law and could speak up for them.

Leaning back in his chair, he smiled and stretched. But his smile turned down when he thought he heard the siren to alert the town's volunteer fire department. He was stand-by only, but he hadn't missed a call yet. He wouldn't tonight, either.

He'd grabbed his jacket and was putting his arms into it when he remembered he had Sophie. He couldn't leave her there alone, and he didn't want to take her to the fire, either. Glancing at his watch, he thought Libby, being a night owl, might be up. If not, he hoped she'd understand that he had no choice. He went to Sophie's room, bundled her in a blanket and grabbed her slippers, then carried her out to his car. The wind was still blowing, which was not a good sign, but it didn't seem to have gotten any colder.

As he drove to Libby's, he hoped it wouldn't take long to drop off Sophie. He still had to drive by the fire station to get his equipment and ask where the fire was.

But as he drew nearer to Libby's, the glow of a fire became brighter. The closer he got, the more cars he saw, parked along the side of the street. And then he saw the flashing lights of the fire engines and police cars. When he was as close as he could get, he realized what was on fire—the duplex where Noah and Libby lived.

Fear left him frozen and unable to think. His chest tightened with almost unbearable pressure and his head began to pound. When someone knocked on his window, he jumped, then looked to see Morgan gesturing for him to roll down his window.

"It doesn't look good," the sheriff said, his face serious.

"Is Libby—" Garrett began, but couldn't finish.

"They're out. I think Libby was the one who called in the fire. But with this wind…"

Garrett nodded. "I have Sophie with me," he said, his voice breaking. "I was on my way over to see if Libby would keep an eye on her while I went to the fire. I didn't expect—"

Soft crying turned his attention to his daughter in the backseat. Instead of speaking, she pointed at the fire.

"It's Libby's house, honey, but she and Noah are okay." He glanced at Morgan, who nodded. "Hang on, and we'll go see them."

After making sure she was well bundled and her slippers wouldn't fall off, Garrett followed Morgan to the ambulance, where he finally found Libby standing nearby, a blanket around her shoulders, while someone checked Noah in the back of the ambulance.

"Libby?" he said.

She spun around at the sound of his voice. "Oh, Garrett."

He hurried to her and, holding Sophie in one arm, he pulled Libby close with his other arm. "Are you all right?"

She nodded and sniffed. "I'm fine. Noah's fine. They just want to check him over." She turned to look at the blaze, licking at tree branches. "But we've probably lost everything."

He felt Sophie move, and gave her an encouraging hug. But before he could say anything, he heard a tiny voice.

"Daddy, is my dollhouse all gone?"

Chapter Seven

Even in the dark, lit only by the flashing lights of emergency vehicles and the glow of the fire, Libby didn't miss the look on Garrett's face when Sophie asked about her dollhouse, and her heart sang with joy. It had been hard to keep from telling him about hearing Sophie speak to Noah, but it was a secret worth keeping, just to see his face when he experienced it for himself.

"Your son is fine, Libby," the young female EMT told her. "Now let me check you over and make sure you didn't breathe in too much smoke."

"I'm okay," Libby insisted. "Really," she

added, seeing the frown of disapproval on the young woman's face. "I was very careful and kept my mouth covered while I woke my son and we were getting out of the apartment."

"Go on with Lucy," Garrett told her. "You need to get checked, no matter what you think."

She didn't have the energy to argue, so she followed Lucy to the ambulance, sitting just inside the big doors in the back. "This really isn't necessary," she attempted.

Lucy slipped the stethoscope in her ears and smiled. "I'll feel better if you let me check, okay?"

Libby nodded and breathed deeply when told to. All the while, she thought about the things they'd lost. They'd had so little to begin with, and now this. Life had begun looking better, especially financially, since she no longer had to pay for child care. Instead of scrimping on other things so Noah could enjoy playing football, she could afford to splurge a little.

Now everything was gone. Or ruined. Furniture, clothes, everything. Somehow she would have to find another place to live and buy the things needed to make it livable for Noah. Just thinking about it brought tears to her eyes.

As Lucy finished checking her, Sheriff Rule

walked up with one of the city councilmen. "Mike Stacy is our fire chief," he explained, introducing the man. "We thought you might want to know what happened. It wasn't your fault, Libby. We want you to know that."

Determined not to cry, she could only nod. Did it really matter if it was or wasn't her fault? If it was, would they sue her? Run her out of town on a rail? She covered her face with her hands and took a deep breath. When she felt calmer, she lowered her hands and looked at the fire chief. "Go ahead, Mr. Stacy."

"There's still some smoldering, but we'll keep an eye on it," he told her. "By morning, you should be able to look through things and see what's salvageable."

Unable to speak in case it would push her over the edge, she nodded again.

"The county fire marshal will be out at some point and make the official determination on the cause, but we're pretty certain it was an electrical fire that started in the wiring in the wall between your place and Mrs. Moran's. Luckily, someone said she's visiting her sister right now. We'll try to get a number for her tomorrow and let her know." He put his hand on Libby's shoulder. "It's an older place and probably hadn't been checked for some time. I'm sorry this had to happen to you, but I'm sure there are people in town who would like to help you."

Libby tried to quietly clear her throat, but failed. "Thank you. I guess I'll know more after we go through things tomorrow."

He nodded and patted her shoulder, his eyes full of sympathy. "We'll need to find a place for you and Noah to stay, at least for tonight."

Before she could even think, Garrett stepped up, still holding Sophie in one arm and the other around her son. "She and Noah will stay with us."

Mike Stacy looked at him and then at Libby. "That would be fine. Whatever you both decide to do."

Libby wasn't convinced it was a good idea. This was a small town and rumors spread like, well, they spread like wildfire. She wouldn't subject Garrett and Sophie to that kind of thing.

Pulling the blanket around her a little tighter, she stood. "There's no need for that, Garrett. We'll find a motel or something, at least for a while, until we can decide what to do next." Not that she thought they had any alternative, now that they had nothing.

The fire chief was called away at that

moment, and Garrett glanced around, then stepped closer to Libby. "I'd be happy to get you a hotel room in Oklahoma City, but have you forgotten that Noah has school to attend?"

She opened her mouth to answer, but closed it quickly. "There must be someplace closer."

"There isn't, so don't argue." He looked down at her son. "Noah, can you stay in my car with Sophie while I help your mom?"

Libby hadn't noticed how shell-shocked Noah looked until then, when he nodded in answer to Garrett. There was nothing to do while Garrett took the two children to his car, so she waited. Maybe it wouldn't hurt to stay at his place tonight. Noah spent so much time there, he'd be comfortable, and she'd just have to deal with it. By morning she might have an idea of what to do next, because right now, she was coming up empty-handed.

She watched as Garrett returned, stopping to speak to Mike Stacy again before joining her. "I know you're concerned with what people will think," he told her, keeping his voice low, "but in a case like this, I think people understand. It isn't going to reflect badly on you."

"I wasn't thinking of me," she said, without thinking. Pressing her lips together, she stared at the ground. "You're the city attorney," she reminded him, looking up at him. "I don't want to jeopardize your position."

"Desperation isn't like that," he insisted.

She thought differently, but didn't say so. There was no use arguing. She was too tired, too confused and too scared. All she could do at that moment was hope she could find another place to live in Desperation and find it quickly.

When they arrived at Garrett's, every muscle in her body ached, but she managed to help get Noah and Sophie inside and calmed down. Noah's shock had worn off, and all he could do was talk about the fire and what had happened. All Libby wanted to do was curl up in a corner somewhere and go to sleep. Maybe if she could do that, when morning came, she'd discover this had all been a bad dream.

"We're going to have to do some shifting," Garrett announced, before Libby could sink to the sofa.

She looked around the room confused. "Shifting?"

"This is a three-bedroom house, but one of those bedrooms is currently my home office."

"Oh," she answered, seeing the problem. Why had she agreed to this in the first place? And why, knowing there wasn't room for four, did he insist? As she thought about it, the more she wished she'd put Noah in the car and driven away.

Garrett took a step toward her, obviously noticing that she was ready to bolt. "Now don't worry," he assured her. "When we redecorated Sophie's room, we decided to wait to get her a new bed. She still has the double bed that Paige used. If you wouldn't mind sleeping with Sophie…"

"No," Libby answered, almost too quickly. "No, of course I wouldn't mind. If Sophie doesn't." But after one look at Sophie, who had tumbled onto one of the big, comfy chairs and was sound asleep, Libby wasn't worried. The little girl was probably out for the night.

Garrett stuffed his hands in his pockets and nodded. "Good. Then I'll take the sofa in the office, and Noah can have my bed."

"Noah can take the sofa in the office, Garrett. There's no reason for you to give up your bed."

"I don't mind."

"But I do," Libby insisted. "Believe me, he's slept on worse." Memories of sleeping in a cramped car in late February, shortly after they'd left Arizona were still vivid. She lifted her chin and straightened her shoulders, determined not to let Garrett win this round. "If you aren't agreeable to that, then we can find someplace else."

Sighing, he shook his head. "I don't want you leaving. It's late and you're tired. If it doesn't work out well tonight, we'll make whatever changes are necessary tomorrow. There are too many other things to think about, Libby. Let's all just get some sleep and tackle what we have to tomorrow."

Libby nodded. He was making sense. Besides, she didn't want to get in her car and drive away. Exhaustion had set in, and there was no telling how long it would take her to find a place to stay, not to mention the cost.

"All right," she agreed. "I guess there's no reason why we shouldn't stay." Except that spending time with Garrett in such close quarters wasn't good for her heart. She'd just have to ignore the way it tripped when he smiled. Or spoke. Or simply stood there and did nothing.

The strong smell of smoke permeated the damp and chill morning. Garrett straightened and rubbed the small of his back, looking around the fire site. Not far away from him, Libby was on her knees, going through the debris in what had once been Noah's bedroom. There was very little left of what had once been their home. The fire had apparently started behind a baseboard between the two apartments, spreading upward. If it had started in the ceiling, there might have been less fire damage to their belongings. But he was only guessing, and it didn't change anything. Libby and Noah had been left with almost nothing.

He walked over to where Libby was going through what appeared to have been a dresser. "Any luck?" he asked.

She glanced up and shook her head. "It's not like he had a lot," she answered, as she moved charred rubble aside. She took a deep breath, which seemed to relax her a little. "I'm sure there are a lot of used clothing stores in Oklahoma City where we can get things to replace some of what we've lost."

"Libby—"

"You know," she said, "it really isn't as bad as it seems. We'll do okay."

As she said it, she looked up at him, and he read the determination in her eyes. No matter what, he had faith that she would get through whatever life threw at her. He suspected she had been doing that for some time. But Libby never talked about her life before Desperation.

Before he even had a chance to assure her

that everything would work out, he noticed Hettie Lambert carefully making her way toward them. He wasn't surprised to see her. Most people in Desperation thought of Hettie as the town matriarch. Her great-great-grandfather, Colonel George Ravenel, had been the first to settle in the area and built a Southern mansion in what then were the wilds of Oklahoma territory. In the past few years, Hettie had turned the Ravenel Mansion into the Shadydrive Retirement Home. The inhabitants of it lovingly referred to it as the Commune, and it included not only those who had retired and no longer wanted the responsibilities of running their own home, but a few younger people who had moved in, as well.

"Oh, Libby," Hettie cried, when she drew closer, "what a mess to have to deal with. We need to get some others out here helping. There's no reason for you to have to do all of this."

Libby stood and turned to smile at Hettie. "There isn't nearly as much work to do as there might appear to be, Hettie, but thank you. I'm nearly done."

When Hettie finally reached her, she took Libby into her arms. "These kinds of things are devastating, I know. But good can come of it, too. Mark my words, there'll be major changes—and all good—in your life."

Libby laughed quietly as Hettie released her. "I'll do that and look forward to it."

"Well," Hettie said, stepping back, "no matter what you might think, there's still a lot to do here. I'm sure I can round up a little help." She glanced at Garrett and smiled, before turning back to Libby. "You give me a list of all the things you're going to need to replace."

Libby lowered her head. "That would be pretty much everything."

"I'm not surprised, considering." Hettie looked around the burnt remains of the duplex, sighing softly. Then she seemed to shake off the sadness of the devastation and turned back to Libby. "Where are you and Noah staying?"

"With Sophie and me," Garrett answered quickly.

Hettie's right eyebrow raised just a tad, but she nodded. "You have room, then."

"Libby is bunking with Sophie, and Noah took the sofa in my office."

"I met little Sophie at Fall Festival," Hettie told Libby, moving away from the business of the fire. "She's a sweetheart."

"She is," Libby said. "I've been so fortunate to get to take care of her while Garrett's at work."

Hettie nodded again. "I heard he was watching Noah in the evenings. What a terrific arrangement for the two of you. It's good that two single parents can help each other."

"We think so," Garrett replied, glancing at Libby.

Hettie leaned closer to Libby. "If you can wait until some time next month," she said, her voice low, but still loud enough that Garrett could hear, "the Marsdens' apartment at the Commune will be available. If you and Noah don't mind living with a bunch of fuddy-duddies, that is."

"Oh, that would be wonderful!" Libby cried.

Garrett couldn't deny the prick of disappointment he felt. Granted, his house was one bedroom short of being enough room for all of them, but that could be remedied. He just didn't know how yet.

"You two could still continue with your babysitting arrangement," Hettie assured them. "Everyone loves it when there are children around. They'd probably spoil both of them."

Garrett cleared his throat, hoping his feelings didn't betray him. "It's good that you may have a place, Libby." He turned to Hettie to explain. "She's been worried she wouldn't be able to find anything."

"Thank you so much, Hettie," Libby said, hugging her. "Now all I have to do is find a way to fill an apartment."

Her hopeful smile hid a sadness that Garrett suspected went deep. "Yes, thanks, Hettie."

"No thanks needed," she said, with a wave of her hand. "That's what friends are for. And if I don't get going, some friends might not be too happy that I'm late." She reached out and took Libby's hand. "Don't you worry, Libby. I mean it. You won't go wanting for anything. This town was born of the disappointment and desperation of people looking for new lives, and it's never failed anyone. It won't fail you."

Garrett watched as tears filled Libby's eyes, and she nodded. "All right, Hettie," she answered. "I promise not to worry. And thank you again."

With a smile of encouragement and a pat on Libby's shoulder, Hettie turned and made her way out of the rubble. As she left, Garrett turned to Libby. "See, it isn't going to be as bad as you thought it would be. Now aren't you glad you didn't leave last night?"

Libby avoided looking directly at him. "I

was only going to leave to find somewhere to stay temporarily."

But Garrett suspected that wasn't the whole truth. Last night he'd believed and still did that she was entertaining the idea of leaving Desperation permanently, although he didn't know why. As far as he knew, she enjoyed living there.

"Hand me the bag," he told her, wishing he knew what to do or say to make her feel better. "I'll take it to your car."

"There isn't much in it," she said, handing the black trash bag to him.

"You need a break. Go on back to my place and clean up, while I go out to the Rocking O and pick up Sophie, then we'll all get some lunch." When Libby started to shake her head, he put his hand on her shoulder. He felt her stiffen beneath it, so he gently pulled it away. "Libby, I'm sorry, but you can spend all day digging through this mess, hoping to find things, but in the end, you're only going to exhaust yourself. That isn't going to solve anything."

She nodded, but didn't look at him. "I know. There are only a few other places I want to check for things. I can do it this afternoon.

And then—" She stopped and swallowed. "And then I'll be done here."

There it was again, that talk that sounded as if she were planning to leave. Well, he wasn't going to let that happen. Not until she could recover from the fire, at least.

"I'll pick you up at my place in twenty to thirty minutes, then," he told her. "Is that enough time?"

"Plenty."

He waited for her to get to her car and start it, and then he drove on to Jules and Tanner's ranch, while she continued to his house. As he pulled in the long drive at the Rocking O, he wondered if he'd ever again see the spunky Libby he'd met at Lou's. It was if the fire had been the last straw for her. But she needed to realize that there was always a way to make things right. She'd already bounced back and found an answer to her child care problems. Somehow he was certain this, too, would end up working out.

"Where are we going?" Libby asked for the second time. She was beginning to lose her patience with Garrett, who was being quite tight-lipped about something. He'd been acting strangely since the fire nearly a week before, and it all made her nervous.

"I told you," he answered, with a sigh of what sounded like exasperation. "We're going to the Chick-a-Lick for dinner, but I have to stop by the council meeting for a few minutes first." Glancing at her as he drove down Main Street, he smiled. "It won't take long."

His answer hadn't changed, and she still didn't feel comfortable with it. It wasn't as if she had any options, except maybe opening the door and jumping out, and she wasn't that crazy, although there had been days lately when she hadn't been so sure that she wasn't.

Hettie had shown up two days after the fire with some shirts, jeans, underwear and socks for Noah. Jules and her friends—Kate, Trish, Nikki and Garrett's sister, Paige—had sent some blue jeans and sweats for her, along with some shirts for work. She didn't really need a lot and appreciated their kindness.

"Looks like they moved the meeting to the opera house," Garrett said as they drove by the city building. He drove a little farther to the corner and pulled into an empty parking space right in front of the renovated building. "How lucky can you get, huh?" he asked, shutting off the engine and opening his door.

Libby climbed out of the car and opened the door for Noah in the backseat, while Garrett retrieved his daughter. Together, they walked to the building and entered the foyer, where the restored ticket booths sat empty.

The long hallway echoed with each step they took, and Libby was tempted to walk on her toes to keep from making so much noise. They passed the door to the Sweet and Yummy Ice Cream Parlor, which was strangely empty and dark. It wasn't yet closing time, she was sure, but the other offices and small businesses were all dark, too. She didn't have a chance to point it out to Garrett, when Sophie made an announcement.

"Daddy, I need to potty."

Garrett came to an immediate stop and looked at her. "Now?"

Sophie nodded.

"Well…" He looked at Libby, who was standing on the other side of his daughter.

"I'll take her," Libby said, taking Sophie's hand and smiling down at her. "Do you know where the ladies' room is?" she asked Garrett.

"I think we just passed it."

She glanced behind her, but didn't see a sign. "All right, we'll find it. You and Noah go on in, and we'll be in when we're done.

We won't be long." She gave Sophie's hand a squeeze. "Will we?"

Sophie shook her head, and they turned back down the hall. By the time they found the restroom, Garrett and Noah had already entered the theater.

It didn't take Sophie long, and they were out in the hallway again within minutes. "It's old in here," Sophie said, sniffing, as they started back down the long hallway.

The building was a bit musty, but Libby didn't mind. "It's very old," she told Sophie. "They used to have fancy plays and operas and all kinds of things here."

"What's an opera?"

Libby tried to think of an explanation Sophie might understand. "Have you ever been to a play where people are on a stage, and there's a story? Kind of like a movie, but with real people." When Sophie shook her head, Libby tried again. "It's where people sing a story."

"Oh."

Libby was fairly certain Sophie still didn't have an idea of what an opera was like or even a play. "Maybe someday we can all go to one."

"I like the zoo," Sophie offered, as they stopped at a set of huge double doors at the end of the wide hall.

Libby smiled at her as she reached for the door. "Maybe we can do that in the spring."

Pulling the heavy door open, she held it for Sophie, and then followed her, making sure the door didn't bang closed. The huge theater was more than half full, but quiet for the number of people in it. She looked around for Garrett and her son, and finally found them hurrying up the side aisle toward her and Sophie.

"What's going on?" she whispered, when she noticed everyone was watching them.

"Come with us." Garrett took Sophie's hand, and led them toward the large stage.

Libby nearly jumped when a microphone screeched feedback, and then the mayor of Desperation spoke. "We're glad you and your son could join us, Libby."

She stared at him, unable to speak. Garrett took her hand and helped her climb the steps to the stage and accompanied her across it to where the mayor was standing at the microphone.

She looked at Garrett, who nodded and smiled, then she looked at the mayor. Inside she was quaking, and she prayed her knees would hold her. "Th-thank you," she finally answered.

"There isn't a person in or around Desperation who didn't hear about the fire that destroyed your home and your belongings," the mayor continued, "and every one of them wanted to help in some way."

Her mouth opened to speak, but nothing came out as she looked out at what seemed to be a sea of people. "I—I don't know what to say," she managed.

The mayor's deep chuckle rumbled through the theater. "We don't expect you to say anything, just accept this—" He turned to Mike Stacy, who was walking onto the stage from behind the curtain, with a large piece of cardboard. "Thank you, Mike," the mayor finished and took the cardboard from him. "Libby, we want you to have this check for five thousand dollars, with more promised in the next few days. Hopefully this will get you back on your feet and able to provide the things you and your son need now and in the near future."

Libby, unable to speak, felt the wet tears slide down her cheeks as she nodded. Her vision blurred as she glanced at Garrett, whose warm smile bathed her in a feeling she'd forgotten. She suddenly realized that throughout everything she'd been through since she'd moved to Desperation, the one thing she'd tried not to do had happened. She was in love with Garrett Miles. All she knew was that she couldn't let that happen, but at that moment she didn't know how to stop it.

Chapter Eight

"We'll have her back this evening," Paige promised as she hustled Sophie out the front door.

Garrett followed them and waved goodbye to his daughter from the porch. "Be good for your Aunt Paige, Sophie, and don't wear out Uncle Tucker," he called.

With a sigh as they drove away, he went back inside and closed the door. Before he could walk to the other side of the room, the doorbell rang.

"Tell him I'll be there in a sec," Noah shouted from the direction of Garrett's office at the end of the hall. "See ya later, Mom," he added, passing the door to the room Sophie and Libby shared.

"Mind your manners," she called after him. "And have a good time."

Garrett moved back quickly as Noah brushed by him, answering Libby. "I will."

The boy was out the door in a flash, and Garrett had to silence a laugh. Noah had wanted to go out to the Bent Tree Boys Ranch to visit his friend Kirby MacGregor, but his mother had a protective streak where he was concerned and wasn't eager to allow the visit.

When Noah had told him in confidence that there were times when a guy needed to spend time with his friends, without his mother, it had been all Garrett could do to keep a straight face. Libby had been hesitant to let Noah spend the day with Kirby, Mac and Nikki MacGregor's adopted son, until Garrett realized it was because of the boys at the Bent Tree Boys Ranch. He'd reminded her that the boys were under Mac and Nikki's care. Jules O'Brien had built the ranch for boys who had slipped through the cracks of the justice system and needed someone who believed in them. That's all it had taken for Libby to give Noah the okay to visit Kirby.

With both children gone for the day, the

house seemed strangely quiet. It had only been ten days since he'd convinced Libby to stay at his house after the fire, but in those ten days, the four of them had settled into a comfortable routine.

Or at least he thought they were settled. Sitting in the living room, watching a football game with the sound muted, while he worked, he could hear Libby moving in the bedroom she shared with Sophie. Every now and then, the door would open, and then quietly close with a soft click. It was beginning to get on his nerves, but he kept himself from saying anything.

When he realized he'd read the same paragraph four times and had completely forgotten about the game, he blew out a breath and counted to five. "Libby," he called, when he reached six, "why don't you come out here?"

He heard the door open, and then she answered, "I'm busy."

"Doing what?"

There was a moment of silence, and then the sound of the door closing. Within seconds, it opened again. "I need to get a drink of water. Or something," she explained as she headed in the direction of the kitchen.

Having had enough of whatever was bothering her, and feeling a little out of kilter himself, he stood and went to the foyer closet and pulled out his tweed jacket and a heavy sweater. "Come on," he called to her, following her to the kitchen.

He found her at the sink, looking out the window, but she jumped and spun around when he spoke. "What?"

"Let's take a walk. You're driving me crazy with whatever is bothering you, and a little exercise wouldn't hurt either of us."

"Oh. Well…"

He stepped into the kitchen and held out the sweater. "I won't take no for an answer."

She hesitated, then finally sighed and took the sweater, but without looking at him. "Is it cold out?"

"Not very," he answered, making sure she walked in the direction of the door. "It was warm and sunny earlier, but I think some clouds rolled in, and now it's a bit overcast."

He looked down at her as he reached for the doorknob. Her furrowed brow and the gnawing of her lower lip were proof of her hesitancy, but she surprised him and walked outside when he opened the door.

He looked at the gray clouds hanging low in the sky. "Good walking weather."

"Is it?"

"Better than snow," he said with a grin.

The hint of a smile turned up the corners of her mouth. "Or hundred degree temps."

"Or sixty mile an hour winds."

The rest of her smile was slow but bright, and she seemed to relax as they stepped off the porch. "I get your point. Are you a walker, then?"

He nodded. "A runner, really. Or was, until we started sharing the child care." He sneaked a look at her to see what her reaction was and found her expression was hard to read.

"I feel like I should be apologizing," she said slowly, then glanced up at him. "But it wasn't my idea to share."

"Exactly, so no apologies necessary. I can always use my lunch hour if I want to get back to it."

"Do you?"

"Want to get back to it?" he asked. When she nodded, he didn't answer immediately. "Until now, I hadn't really thought about it, but, yeah, I think I might. What about you?"

They'd come to the corner, and she shook her head. "I'll pass," she said, as he steered them to the right. "I get enough walking at work."

They came to the end of another block, this time without speaking. It was one of those times that he didn't feel words were needed. He had his own thoughts to mull over and assumed she did, too.

"But you know…"

He looked at her. "What?"

She started to go on, then stopped and shook her head, a spot of pink glowing on each cheek. "Nothing."

"No, what?"

"Nothing, really."

"You had a thought. Are you afraid to share it?"

She stopped and turned, looking up at him. "Why would I be afraid?"

His heartbeat kicked up a notch as he gazed down at her. "That's a very good question. Why would you be?"

She didn't answer and instead turned to continue walking. The silence had been easy between them, but now he felt her drawing away. He'd learned that asking too much would cause her to close some invisible door, and she'd find a way to put distance—physical distance—between them. So instead of saying anything, he led her toward the outskirts of town, to the Commune, where Hettie had told her there might soon be an apartment open that she could rent.

"I've never been by here," Libby said, when he explained where they were. "It's…"

"Great?"

She turned to him and chuckled. "Well, that's one word, but not exactly what I was thinking." When she turned back, he heard her whisper, "Wow."

"You won't even have to cook."

"Really?" she asked, looking over her shoulder.

"Freda does all the cooking."

"And who is Freda?"

He explained the story he'd been told of how Morgan's uncle, Ernie Dolan, had met Freda years before during his travels in Sweden, and how she'd longed to come to America. He brought her back to the States, and she settled in New York. Later, when Hettie decided to reinvent her stately family home, she'd given the task of overseeing Shadydrive to Ernie, and he brought Freda to Desperation as the official Commune cook.

"So Sheriff Rule is a native of Desperation?" she asked.

Garrett shook his head. He knew the story of how Morgan had come to town after his partner on the police force in Miami had been killed during a drive-by shooting. "That story is for another time. So what do you think of the place?" he asked, nodding at the three-story mansion.

"It's beautiful," she answered, just as the sky opened up and let loose with a drenching rain. Instead of hurrying to the big house in front of them, she turned her face up, the rain pelting her.

He flipped up the collar of his jacket at the sudden wet chill and took her arm. "Let's get out of this," he said, intending to take her to a drier spot, wherever that might be.

Instead, she shook her head. "I won't melt."

"You're getting soaked."

She moved to look at him, a smile lighting her face. "I won't melt, Garrett," she said again. "I'm not made of sugar."

He was certain she'd lost her mind, and he slipped an arm around her waist, intending to lead her to shelter. "You could catch a cold or something. Let's find a dry spot to wait this out."

But instead of allowing him to lead her away, she turned to face him. "You aren't afraid of a little rain, are you?"

"Not in the least, if you aren't." Wrapping her in both arms, he spun around in a circle. "Now who's afraid?" he teased.

She tipped her head back, laughing as they spun, then suddenly she pulled out of his grasp and took off running. "Wait!" he shouted, but she didn't even slow down. All he could do was wonder what had gotten into her and follow as she picked up speed.

They were only a few blocks from home, when he'd had enough. He'd caught up with her and, reaching out, took her arm and turned her around to face him.

"Talk to me, Libby," he said, looking into the depths of her amber eyes. "What is it?" he whispered, afraid he would scare her away.

"It's nothing," she answered, and tried to break free, but he held her tight.

When he turned her face with one finger so he could look into her eyes again, he saw the sparkle of tears. Cupping her cheek with one hand, he pulled her closer with his other. "Won't you let me help?"

Her sigh seemed to come from the depths of her, but she didn't look away. Tears mixed with raindrops as they made a path down her cheek, and then her eyes slowly drifted shut. Without thinking, he lowered his head and pressed his lips to hers. He felt her start to pull away, and then she seemed to fold herself into him.

* * *

"You better get out of those wet clothes, and I'll get a fire started."

With her teeth chattering from the cold and feeling too stunned to speak, Libby silently passed Garrett and went through the front door he held open. She couldn't believe she'd let him kiss her. No. It was more than that. She'd participated. She'd kissed him back! What had she been thinking?

Finally in the privacy of the room she shared with Sophie, she stripped out of her wet clothes and pulled one of the extra blankets from the closet, wrapping herself in it. Still shivering and unable to stop, she sat on the edge of the bed and dropped her head to her hands. Nothing made sense.

She had obviously gone insane, she decided. The fire at her duplex had been too much, and she must have reached a breaking point, standing out there in the rain. Yes, she'd admitted to herself that she was in love with Garrett, but she had more common sense than to let herself get swept away. Or she'd thought she did.

She hadn't had any common sense when she married Eric, but he'd swept her off her feet and treated her like a princess. Her parents had been thrilled when he proposed. After all, the

Cabrera family owned the biggest real estate business in Phoenix and, to her family, it was a step up from even their country club world in Tucson. Libby had never wanted for anything as a child, and she certainly wouldn't as Eric Cabrera's wife. Everyone was excited and happy.

If only they knew. But they didn't. She hadn't told anyone the first time he'd hit her. After that, it became her dark secret. The trips to the hospital, the dislocated jaw, the broken rib, the knife he'd used to slice into her—just enough to make her bleed, he'd said. She'd never even told Suze, who'd been her friend since college. The only person who knew was Noah, and she prayed that he'd been young enough to have forgotten what he'd seen. Eric had been careful, never leaving marks that could be easily noticed, and rarely did he do anything when Noah was present. But she feared there had been a time or maybe two when Noah had seen.

Water dripped from her hair, bringing Libby back to the present. She went for a towel, making certain she was quiet. Returning to the bedroom, she reached to the back of the high shelf in the closet and nearly lost her balance. With her fingertips, she finally found the shoebox that had been hidden in the wheel well of her car and eased it forward, until she could grab it.

Sinking to the floor, she opened the box and pulled out the disposable cell phone. She stared at it, wondering if this would be her undoing. She hadn't spoken to her parents since she and Noah had left Phoenix. There was no doubt in her mind that they were worried. She was their baby, younger by nine years than her brother. He had come along fairly late in their parents' lives, and Libby even later. Her parents deserved to know that she and Noah were all right.

But she had to be careful. She had to make sure the call wouldn't be traced, in case Eric was having their phone tapped. Pressing the code to hide any information she possibly could, she then punched in the familiar number. After five rings, someone picked up.

"Hello?"

Libby closed her eyes and breathed a silent sigh. Just hearing her mother's voice helped to calm her. "Mom? It's me."

"Lauren? Oh, dear! Is it really you? Honey, come here, it's our Lauren."

"I only have a second, Mom. I just want you to know that Noah and I are fine."

"But where are you? When are you coming home?"

Libby ignored the questions. "You have to promise me something, Mom. You and Daddy both."

"Promise? Promise what?"

"Just say you'll promise."

"Yes, yes, of course. Whatever. Anything."

In her mind, Libby could see her mother holding the phone, her father nearby and the frantic looks between them. "Promise that you won't tell anyone—not *anyone*—that I called."

"But what about—"

"Not anyone."

"All right, I promise. We both do. But—"

"Goodbye, Mom. I love you, and Daddy, too. Tell him that." Slowly, she pushed the button and disconnected the call.

She tried not to think that she might have done the wrong thing. If she could trust them not to contact Eric, she would go home, but she couldn't. They thought the world of him, and they'd never accept the truth if she told them. It was better this way.

A hot shower followed in the hope it would chase the chill that had settled into her, and the hot spray helped clear her mind, if not warm her soul. After slipping into some soft, comfy sweats, she dried her hair and tried not to think of what she needed to say to Garrett.

She'd known since the apartment fire that she couldn't stay in Desperation much longer. She might love Garrett, but she was damaged goods, and nothing would come of any kind of relationship with him or with anyone. The outside scars were hidden so others couldn't see, but it was the inside ones that would eventually betray her. She could never again trust her own judgment. And Eric would never allow another man in her life, of that she was certain. Leaving Desperation was her only option.

There was a light tap on the door, and she jumped in response, then did her best to calm her racing heart.

"The fire's roaring, and I've made some hot tea," Garrett said from the other side of the door. "Would you like some?"

"That sounds great, thank you," she answered, hoping something in her voice didn't give away how raw her emotions were at the moment. "I'll be out in a minute."

"Meet you in the living room, then."

She'd made a mistake by letting him see her reaction to the kiss, but it might not be too late to fix that. She'd simply have to act as if it hadn't meant anything. That it was perfectly normal for them to share a kiss in the rain. He must never know how she truly felt.

Everything appeared normal when she stepped out of the bedroom. The living room wasn't lit brightly, but it rarely was, and the blaze in the fireplace added an additional warm glow. The soft rug that always lay in front of the fireplace was still there, but now the coffee table had been added, along with two cups of tea placed at opposite ends.

"I was going to offer you some wine," he said. "And the look on your face is exactly why I didn't," he added, when she turned to look at him.

She laughed, making light of it, and when he nodded to the far end of the table, she sat cross-legged on the pillow he'd placed there. "I have to admit it would surprise me if you had," she replied. "I've never even seen you with a beer at Lou's."

"Too many wild nights when I was younger." He settled on the pillow at the other end. "I pretty much gave it up."

"So you don't drink at all?"

"Not often and not much."

"There's nothing wrong with that."

"My thoughts, exactly."

She took a sip of the tea and began to feel

warmer. "What time do you think Noah and Sophie will be back?"

He gave her a sheepish glance. "Noah called and asked me to tell you that he's been invited to stay for dinner. I didn't think you'd mind."

She wasn't sure she liked that he hadn't called her to the phone, but she remembered she might have been in the shower at the time. "No, I don't mind."

"I'm glad I didn't screw that up," he said with a nervous chuckle.

The last thing she wanted was for him to think she was an unreasonable mother. She did keep a watchful eye on Noah, but she had her reasons...reasons she couldn't share.

"As long as he isn't there too late," she answered, "and the roads don't get too bad, what with all this rain, it's okay."

With the back of his hand, he wiped his forehead. "Whew!"

She laughed again, and they both became quiet, focusing on the fire crackling warmly beside them. Sometime later, he stood. "More tea?" he asked.

"No, but it did warm me. Thank you." When he took her empty cup, she scrambled to her feet. "Let me," she said, reaching for his cup.

"There's no reason you should do all the work. We share, remember?"

He relinquished it without an argument. "I'll get the table moved."

Alone in the kitchen, she closed her eyes and sighed. If she were honest with herself, she'd admit that she wanted to spend the evening with him, no matter whether it was right or wrong. She'd already decided to leave at the end of the week. She couldn't tell him, and she'd never get the chance to tell him why or even goodbye. Why shouldn't she enjoy herself until then?

Garrett had tried not to stare at Libby when she left the room. He'd never seen any woman who looked as great in a pair of sweats as she did. A pair of sweats! They weren't even tight, but they moved in the right places when she did. He couldn't think of anything at that moment that she'd look better in. Except maybe one of his shirts and nothing else.

Chiding himself for even thinking something like that, he focused on moving the coffee table back to its original place, trying to erase that image of Libby walking to the kitchen.

It was getting more difficult every day to regard her as a friend and nothing more. He'd wanted her before he'd kissed her, and now he wanted her more. The shared child care that had been his idea was now what kept him from approaching her. Even after their walk and everything that had happened, he wasn't sure how she'd react to anything more than the innocent flirting they'd enjoyed before they'd become babysitters for each other's child. The last thing he wanted to do was frighten her. At any other time, he would have let her know how he felt. But now that she was living in his house, he didn't feel it was right to pursue her. But, damn, it wasn't going to be easy not to.

When she returned, she hesitated slightly, looking first at the fireplace hearth, where he'd left the two pillows on the floor, to where he stood near the sofa. "I didn't know if the tea took the chill off completely, so..." He glanced toward the fire.

Her smile was as sweet as always. "The fire is fine. Perfect."

He joined her near the hearth. "Having grown up with Chicago winters, I've always thought there's something comforting about a fire."

She lowered herself to the pillow. "As long as it isn't a burning apartment."

"Right." He settled on the floor near her.

"But it's turned out okay," he added, thinking of the generosity of the town's citizens.

She nodded, but didn't look directly at him. "Yes, it has." She finally glanced his way and smiled at him. "I only wish you'd given me some warning the other night."

"You wouldn't have gone if I'd told you."

Her laugh was soft and gentle as she ducked her head. "You're right. I wish I had a way to thank everyone."

He considered it. "I think just being you and staying in Desperation is all the thanks they expect."

For a brief moment, she pressed her lips tightly together, and then she raised her head, smiling. "Maybe so."

They sat in comfortable silence, watching the flames, and Garrett wished he knew what she was thinking. He was glad she couldn't read *his* mind at that moment. "Why hasn't a beautiful woman like you married again?" he asked, voicing only a little of his thoughts.

She shrugged as she continued to stare at the fire in front of them. "Not a lot of men are interested in a ready-made family."

"It might be easier—"

"Not necessarily."

"You like being single, then?"

She turned slowly and offered him a look that told him he was treading on thin ice. "In a word, yes."

Not knowing how to reply, he nodded and shifted his position, bracing one hand on the floor, so he could focus on the fire, as she had.

"Most of the time," she added, her voice a whisper.

Surprised, he watched her for a moment before he spoke. "Care to explain?"

"Not really," she answered with a shake of her head and a slight smile. "What about you?"

"Do I like being single?" he asked.

She nodded.

"I haven't given it any thought lately. And now with Sophie here, well, let's just say I have some things I need to get used to."

"Yes, you do," she said, softly. She leaned toward him and placed her hand on his. "You're a good dad, Garrett. Don't ever let anyone tell you that you aren't."

All he could do was nod as his attention moved from her hand on his to her eyes.

"To be honest, I wasn't sure you would be able to handle it," she continued, obviously oblivious to what her touch was doing to him.

He turned his hand over and held hers, rubbing his thumb gently over her soft skin. "I couldn't have done it without you, Libby. You showed me what a good parent is. Not only are you an excellent mother, you're a good teacher."

Without thinking, he leaned forward and kissed her, softly, gently, not wanting to frighten her, yet half expecting her to pull away.

She didn't.

He deepened the kiss.

She sighed, and he heard a catch in her breath. The sound nearly pushed him over the edge of sanity. He didn't know how, but he managed to slowly stretch himself out on the floor and took her with him. Side by side, her head resting on his arm, he slowly ran his finger down her cheek. He moved to nibble her earlobe and felt the shiver that went through her. Kissing his way along her delicate jaw, he breathed in the soft scent of her, branding it in his memory.

He pulled her on top of him, never breaking the gaze they shared. His hands at her waist, he slipped them under her fleece top and touched the warm skin beneath it. When she didn't deny him the pleasure, he touched every inch of her back, memorizing the feel of it.

But something was odd, and his hands stilled for a moment at the feel of tiny ridges. Moving his hands over her sides, his thumbs grazing her waist and slowly inching upward…until he felt something even odder. "Have you broken a rib at some time?" he asked.

He could've sworn he felt her stiffen for the briefest of moments, but she pressed her lips to his and whispered, "Several years ago. A wreck."

"The scars, too?"

Instead of answering him, she kissed him, deeply and slowly, taking his breath away and causing his heart to pound. In one smooth movement, he turned them over and gazed down into her surprised eyes, before capturing her lips again and cupping her breast in his hand. He hadn't planned this. He didn't know how far it would go. But he wasn't going to stop now. Not unless—

Her hands gripped his shirt, and then he realized she was pushing at him, not pulling him closer. He pulled back and saw panic in her eyes. "I'm sorry, Libby," he whispered. "I didn't mean—"

"It's all right," she said, moving away. "But… I… I'm sorry, Garrett. I can't."

Before he had a chance to respond, she was gone.

Chapter Nine

Garrett sat in front of the fire, completely losing track of time as he pondered what had happened with Libby. Had he assumed too much? Had he frightened her? If so, why? He hadn't gotten what he called Don't Touch signals from her, and he'd tried to be very aware of how she responded. Wasn't that what he was supposed to do? Granted, it had been a while since he'd been with a woman. He hadn't dated in more than a year. His life was too busy, and the last woman he'd taken to dinner had been, well, a disappointment.

The sound of a knock brought him back to the present, and he turned to see Sophie walk in the front door with Paige. Still sitting on the floor in front of the fire, Garrett nodded and got to his feet. "Did you have a good time with Aunt Paige?" he asked his daughter.

"We wented to the new house," she said in a rush, her eyes big and round. "Unca Tucker showed me the orchward and the kissy stuff in the trees."

Garrett looked to Paige for an explanation. "Kissy stuff?"

"Mistletoe," Paige answered with a grin.

"Ah!"

Paige moved toward the door. "I need to get back home. Tucker's coming by to talk about colors and things for the house. Thank you for loaning us Sophie again. She never fails to make me smile, and Tucker adores her."

"Me, too," Garrett replied, and put his hand on his daughter's head. When she looked up at him with a big grin, he couldn't help but smile back. "See you soon," he told his sister.

When Paige was gone, Garrett asked Sophie if she'd eaten, and she assured him she had, complete with an explanation of everything she'd had to eat at Paige's and later with Tucker.

She yawned and he checked the clock. It was close to seven-thirty, and he expected

Noah to be back soon. "I guess it's bedtime," he told her. Her answer was a sad nod as he took her to her bedroom.

Hesitant to bother Libby, he knocked softly on the closed door. When there was no answer, he knelt in front of Sophie. "Do you know where your pajamas are?"

Her somber face moved up and down in another nod. "Under my pillow."

"Oh." He considered the problem that she might have getting them, without waking Libby, but decided he didn't have many choices. "Libby is asleep, so be as quiet as you can, then you can change in my bedroom and sleep in my bed. How's that?"

"Will you tuck me in?"

His daughter had come to mean the world to him. "Of course, I will."

His answer seemed to please her as she hurried into the almost-dark bedroom, and he waited, holding his breath, until she reappeared with her pajamas. "Good job," he told her and gave her a thumbs-up as she continued down the hall to his bedroom. "Can you reach the light switch?"

"If I stand on my tippy toes," she answered, and disappeared into the room.

He watched as the light went on, then the

door closed. Minutes later, she called to him, "I'm ready now, Daddy."

As it always did when she called him Daddy, his heart skipped a beat. He'd never known the kind of love he had for Sophie, and he never wanted to lose it or her.

True to his word, he tucked her in, kissed her good-night and returned to the living room just as Noah came in the front door. When Noah asked about his mom, Garrett explained that she'd gone to bed early and was sleeping. Feeling a bit guilty, he was relieved when Noah accepted the answer without question.

"Did you and Kirby have a good time?"

"Yeah, he's cool," Noah answered. "And it's great that he gets to go to school in Desperation, instead of staying at the Bent Tree all the time."

"I'm guessing that's because he's not officially one of the boys at the ranch, but Mac and Nikki's son now."

"I guess." Noah covered a yawn and slung his bag over his shoulder. "I still have a little math homework to finish, so I guess I'll get to it."

"Okay," Garrett replied. "If you need any help, let me know."

"Sure will."

After putting the cups he and Libby had used into the dishwasher and pretending to straighten the kitchen and living room, Garrett finally gave in and checked on Sophie. While in his room, he retrieved a pair of pajama bottoms, then checked on Noah, who he found sleeping soundly on the sofa in the office. He changed into his pajamas and grabbed a spare blanket and pillow from the linen closet in the hall, then he took them all to the living room.

It took a while to finally fall asleep, the evening playing itself over and over enough times for Garrett to memorize every word and touch, but he finally fell into a fitful sleep. He was awakened early by the smell of coffee. Barely able to open his eyes, he caught a glimpse of Libby leaving a cup for him on the coffee table. Grateful, he sat up until his mind was clear enough to think, picked up the cup and headed to the kitchen, ready to apologize to Libby for the night before.

He found her at the table, dressed in jeans and a T-shirt, with *The Oklahoman,* Oklahoma City's newspaper, spread out in front of her. "Are you—" He cleared the morning frog from his throat. "Are you all right?"

She raised her head and nodded. "I owe you an apology."

"No, you don't."

"Yes," she insisted, a stubborn glint in her eyes as she squared her shoulders. "I want you to know that I'm sorry for the way I reacted."

He shook his head and pulled out the chair next to her. "No, it was my fault. I went too far, too fast and—"

"Garrett, it wasn't you. It's me. I was the one who—"

"It isn't your fault, Libby." He settled stiffly on the chair, ready to make his case if necessary.

"But I should have—" Shaking her head, she lowered it. "Look," she continued, "it's time to get the kids up. This will have to keep." Her sigh was deep as she regarded him with eyes sad and serious. "Can we forget about it, at least for now?"

"Sure." He didn't see that he had much of a choice. She obviously wasn't willing to discuss it, and he wouldn't be much of a gentleman if he pushed the issue.

"Thanks."

As she folded the paper and stood, he glanced at the clock and realized it was later than he'd thought. "I need to get going. Early appointment. Can you—"

"I think I'll let Sophie sleep in this morning," Libby said, picking up her coffee cup and carrying it to the sink. She glanced out the window, where wan sunlight tried to shine into the room. "Could you drop Noah at school? It's still pretty soggy out there and he's almost ready."

"Of course." It was clear that what had happened the evening before was now in the past. Trying to talk to her about it would be useless. And maybe she was right. Maybe they should just move on and see where a little more time might take them. He only wished he knew where that might be.

He had no doubt now that he'd fallen in love with Libby. But he wasn't sure she was ready to hear it. Should he tell her? Or would it be better to wait a little longer? He just didn't know.

"How was your nap?" Libby asked Sophie, when the little girl entered the kitchen.

Dressed in her favorite pink shirt, decorated with colorful cartoon characters, the four-year-old rubbed her eyes and yawned. "'Kay. Is Noah home yet?"

Glancing at the clock, Libby shook her head. "Not yet. Not too much longer, though. Would you like some milk and cookies?"

Sophie nodded and climbed onto the tall stool at the table. Crayons and paper were kept there for her, and she reached for them. "I'm going to draw a pitcher of our family," she announced.

Our family. The words hit Libby like a ton of bricks as she poured a glass of milk. Leaving Desperation meant leaving Sophie, the one thing she hated more than anything, but she didn't have a choice. She and Noah would be leaving soon. In the four days since she had stopped herself and Garrett from going too far, she hadn't changed her mind. In fact, she was more determined that leaving was the right thing to do. Not what she wanted to do, but the right thing.

With only two days left until the day she planned to hit the road for places yet unknown, she'd already boxed up as much of her belongings and Noah's as she could, without causing suspicion. Because of the fire, they didn't have much, but her trunk was nearly full. She'd find some time to put the rest in the car before Saturday morning. At least that was the plan. She tried not to think too much about it.

"You have yellow hair," Sophie announced.

Libby filled a small plate with cookies and took it and the milk to the table. Glancing at the drawing, she touched a strand of Sophie's hair, enjoying the silkiness of it. "And you have pretty brown hair," she replied with a smile.

Sophie looked up at her. "Is it really yellow?"

Taken aback for a brief moment, Libby smiled. "My hair? Yes, it's always been yellow."

Sophie sighed. "Sometimes my mommy made hers yellow, but it always got a big stripe down the middle."

Stripe? And then Libby realized she was talking about roots of darker hair that had grown out. Garrett hadn't described Sophie's mother to her, but studying the little girl now, she saw a lot of Garrett.

"I forgot my teddy bears," Sophie suddenly announced and slid to the floor from the tall stool.

Since the fire and loss of her dollhouse, Sophie's two bears had once again become her most treasured toys. Garrett had mentioned that he was looking for another dollhouse to replace the one that was destroyed and planned to give it to Sophie for Christmas. Libby couldn't stop the thought from entering her mind that she and Noah would be far away by then, and she wouldn't be around to see Sophie's joy.

Before the sadness could overwhelm her, the doorbell rang. Her first thought, as she went to the door, was to wonder why the door was locked and that Noah must have forgotten his key. Reaching for the knob, she pulled the door open with a smile, expecting to see her son.

"It's just like you to shack up with some guy."

With her reactions slowed by shock, Libby didn't close the door fast enough, and her ex-husband wedged himself in the doorway. "Go away," she whispered, as he shoved his way inside.

"Is that any way to treat your husband?"

She stepped back, putting as much space between them as possible, but the wall in the entryway stopped her. "You aren't my husband, so just get out."

Eric's eyes bored into her, as his mouth stretched into a sickening smile. "Did you think I would let you get away with taking my son?"

Hearing the threatening note in his voice, she didn't answer, nor did she look away. There was no telling what he might do if she did. But if she could take a step to her right, she could make a run for it. Maybe.

But how far would she get? And how could she leave Sophie by herself?

Sophie!

Her heart pounded, but she couldn't let on that there was anyone else in the house. She couldn't believe Eric would do anything to the little girl, but she could also see that he was in a rage and there was no way to know what he might do.

"Where's Noah?" he asked, inches from her face.

She was shaking inside so badly, she could barely breathe, but she refused to let him see how frightened she was. "He isn't here."

His dark eyebrows arched high over nearly black eyes, and he looked past her and over her shoulder to the living room. She prayed that Sophie wasn't anywhere to be seen, but she couldn't guess how long it had been since the little girl had left the table to get her teddy bear. And she couldn't be sure that Sophie would know to keep out of sight.

"Where is he?" Eric asked, pinning her with his stare again.

She wished she could see a clock and feared

Noah would be home any minute. If she could just get rid of Eric… "School," she answered.

"School?"

The perplexed expression on his face nearly made her laugh, but she did her best to add a haughty note to her voice, instead. "He's nine years old, Eric. He's not a little boy anymore. Or don't you remember?"

Doubt and confusion clouded his eyes, but he nodded. "Of course I remember."

Thinking quickly, she added, "He was going home with a friend to study, I think. If you come back later—"

"You underestimate me, Lauren. I'm surprised. But I'm not that foolish."

Feeling frustrated and frightened, she tried to think of something else she could say that might send him away. But she knew he was on his game, and he'd never believe anything she said, even if it was the truth.

She nearly died when she heard the sound of footsteps on the porch and hoped Eric didn't hear them, too. She should have known better. Eric's senses were always heightened when he was in a rage. The sound distracted him, and when he turned, she quickly eased around the corner, away from him. He didn't try to stop her, but she glanced out the heavy door that he hadn't yet closed and saw Noah standing in the open doorway.

Run, Noah! her mind screamed, but she remained silent and turned her attention to Eric. If he made a move to harm Noah, she wasn't sure she could stop herself from doing whatever it took to keep her son safe.

"Come in, come in, son," Eric said, making way for Noah to step inside the house.

Libby felt Noah look at her before doing what Eric had told him to. Tears began to fill her eyes when she realized her small son hadn't forgotten the past as she'd hoped he had.

"What are you doing here?" Noah asked.

Libby detected the contempt in his voice and hoped Eric hadn't noticed. They'd been divorced for five years, when Noah had come home with a black eye after a scheduled visit with his father. She'd asked Noah what had happened, but he refused to talk about it. A week later, she'd been served with court papers. Eric had filed for sole custody. She'd been enraged and frightened and hired a lawyer, determined to keep her son from Eric, once and for all. But the judge—a close friend of the Cabrera family—had thrown out her claim and the little evidence she dared show of abuse and given Eric the custody he'd asked for. It was then that she'd gone to the group who'd helped her and Noah escape. She was breaking the law. She'd kidnapped her son.

Eric looked from her to Noah, who was now moving to her side. "I came for a visit," Eric said with a smile that frightened her. "To say hello and see how you are."

"We're fine," Noah answered, standing tall, "so you can leave."

The look on Eric's face was almost a sneer as he glanced at Libby. "I see your mother has been telling you lies."

"Mom doesn't lie. She doesn't need to. I remember—"

When Eric took a quick and bold step toward Noah, his hand drawn back, Libby stepped between them. "Don't even try it."

Garrett wedged the phone between his cheek and shoulder and propped his elbows on his desk. "I don't know how to thank you, Miss Foster."

"It's Tracy, please. Just make sure Shana never gets that little girl back again. She'd stay out all night, leaving Sophie alone. I'd go over and check on her, and sometimes I'd even stay until Shana came home, but I couldn't always do that. And I worried. You know?"

Wiping a hand down his face, he took the phone in his hand. "Yes, and thank you. I have legal papers that Shana will have to sign, giving up all parental rights. Now that I know where she's gone, I can have her served with them."

"I'm glad I could help," the young woman said. "And if you remember, would you tell Sophie hello for me?"

"Of course. And again, thank you."

When the call ended, he hung up the phone and let out a long, relieved sigh. Tracy Foster had given him all the information he needed to find Shana. It had taken more than a month to track someone down who knew something, but it had finally happened.

Stretching out his arms, he smiled. Excitement and relief surged through him. This was the news they'd been waiting for. He needed to share it with Libby. She'd be as excited as he was.

Tootie poked her head in his open door. "Mayor wants to see you."

"I can't right now, Tootie," he said, standing and pulling on his tweed jacket. "Tell him I left early."

"No can do."

Garrett looked at her and frowned. "But—"

"Any other time I'd help you out, but he's in

a bad mood today, and I'm not risking a white lie." She smiled. "Not even for you."

Although he was eager to get home and tell Libby his news, skipping out when the mayor insisted on seeing him was a bad idea. He returned Tootie's smile. "All right. Tell him I'll be right there."

Tootie disappeared, and Garrett picked up the phone, dialing his home number. After listening to it ring several times, he shrugged and hung up. Libby must have decided to walk to the school with Sophie to meet Noah. He'd deal with the mayor as quickly as possible and maybe make it home at the same time they did.

His meeting with the mayor took longer than he'd thought. There was a battle going on in town over proposed zoning changes, and the council was going to need a more intense study on the legalities of them. Garrett was able to assure the mayor that he'd have the necessary information in time for the next council meeting.

On the drive home, he started making plans for a celebration. Of course they couldn't tell Sophie why they were celebrating, but Libby could help him with that. He knew that someday he would have to tell his daughter about all of it, but he hoped he'd be able to do it in a way that wouldn't make her sad. If he was lucky, Libby would be there to help him do that, too. Just the thought made him smile again.

As he drove down the last block to his house, he noticed a strange car in his drive. Pulling into the driveway next to it, he was puzzled by the Arizona tags. He was aware that Libby had lived in Arizona and wondered if this was a visit from someone in her family. She'd never mentioned any family, but that didn't mean anything. She rarely talked about her past. As far as he was concerned, if she wasn't a convict or breaking the law, her past didn't matter.

Feeling better than he had in days, he stepped onto the porch and through his open front door, Libby's name on his lips, ready to call out. But he was immediately puzzled by what he saw in his living room.

A man he didn't know and couldn't remember ever seeing, quickly turned around, obviously as surprised to see him as he was to see the man.

"Hello," Garrett greeted him, glancing at Libby. Something in her eyes caused him to study the stranger, who was nearly as tall as him, with dark hair and a lean build. Something about him was familiar, but he didn't know why. "I don't believe we've met," Garrett said, offering the man his hand.

Stepping forward, the man took his hand with a grip that left no doubt he wanted to prove himself. Just the kind Garrett hated. Macho to the core, without a thought for anyone but himself. The guy's smile said the same.

"Eric Cabrera," the man said, glancing at Libby.

Puzzled, Garrett smiled and pulled his hand out of Cabrera's grasp.

"I came to see my boy," Cabrera said.

"Your boy?" Garrett repeated. He didn't understand what was going on. Libby wasn't saying a word, just standing in front of Noah as if she was protecting him. But then she did have that protective nature, sometimes almost smothering, he reminded himself.

"Who are you?" he asked.

"I'm her husband," the man said, his entire demeanor impatient.

"Ex-husband," Libby said.

Garrett looked around the room, trying to assess what the situation might be. There was so much tension in the air, he could almost taste it. Libby's eyes, wide and almost devoid of emotion, were pinned on her ex-husband, the man she had said was out of the picture. Her face was pale, and there wasn't even a ghost of a smile as she stared at the man. It was obvious she was not only surprised but not at all happy to see him. But Garrett could understand that a father would want to see his son, and as far as he knew, the guy hadn't stepped a foot in Desperation since Libby had moved there.

His eyes were drawn to the hallway, where he finally noticed Sophie, standing perfectly still in the afternoon shadows, her eyes wide as she appeared to squeeze the stuffing out of her teddy bears. Their gazes met, but instead of stepping out and into the room, she hugged the wall and shook her head slightly.

The tension was almost too much to bear, and he guessed that was why Sophie wouldn't come out. "Why don't we all sit down?" he suggested to the others, hoping to ease the situation.

"I was just leaving," Cabrera said, but he didn't move.

"Sorry to hear that," Garrett replied, not meaning it at all. Something wasn't right.

Eric Cabrera turned to Libby. "I'll be taking Noah with me."

Libby stepped back but didn't turn, her hands reaching behind her for her son. "No."

"I didn't come here to argue with you about

it," her ex answered, his voice low, almost private, but loud enough that Garrett could hear. "I came here to take Noah home. And you, too, if you want to come with us."

"Neither of us is leaving."

"That's not what the law says."

A flash of panic crossed her face, but she didn't answer.

Garrett cleared his throat, gaining Cabrera's attention. "What law is that?"

"You mean she hasn't told you?"

Glancing at Libby, Garrett felt a sudden uneasiness. "Told me what?"

"Go ahead, Lauren. Tell him."

Lauren?

Seconds went by, but she didn't speak, and Cabrera turned his attention to Garrett. "She kidnapped Noah almost nine months ago."

Garrett stared at Libby. "Kidnapped?"

"She left the state with him. I'd been given sole custody by the judge."

Cold washed over Garrett. All this time, he'd assumed Noah's father was aware of his whereabouts. Or at the very least that Libby had full custody of their son. He'd never felt the need to question her. She was a good mother. An excellent mother.

At least that's what he'd thought. He hadn't

wanted to pry. He hadn't felt there was a need. She was just like Shana. She'd lied and deceived him.

He was surprised when she finally spoke. "I'm sorry, Garrett. I never expected you to be pulled into this, but I won't let him have Noah. I can't."

"You lied to me. You're no better than Shana," he said through stiff lips, his head throbbing. After taking a deep breath to get a grip on his anger, he called to his daughter. "Sophie, come here, please."

Hesitating at first, she walked slowly to him. He put his arm around her and pulled her close, then faced Libby. "I don't care what the two of you decide to do about Noah. I won't go to the sheriff about this. Not yet, anyway. But I want you all out of here in thirty minutes. And don't come back."

Without looking at Libby, he took Sophie's hand and led her to the door. As far as he was concerned, Libby—or whatever her name was—was on her own, and he never wanted to see her again.

Chapter Ten

Libby's eyes stung with unshed tears as she watched Garrett and Sophie walk out the door. How had it come to this? Why had she let it get this far? Maybe if she'd told him why she'd left Phoenix, he might understand. But she'd been afraid he would turn her in. Would he have helped her if he'd known? She'd never know.

"Get your things."

Libby heard but didn't respond to Eric, too lost to care.

"Now!"

But she wasn't too lost to recognize the threat in Eric's demand, and she felt a sudden surge of strength. "I told you, Noah isn't going anywhere with you."

Eric's smile was void of kindness. "And I said he is. In fact, both of you are."

Cold dread hit Libby like a punch, but she wouldn't back down. "No."

Eric took a step forward. "Do you think I'm crazy enough to leave you here now?"

Instead of retreating, she held her ground. "There's no reason—"

"There's every reason. I know you never looked at another man after the divorce. All that time. You knew I'd know everything you did, everyone you even spoke to. But it didn't take you long to find a lover, once you were out of Arizona and out of sight."

"We aren't lovers," she insisted. "We share child care. That's why I'm here. His daughter—"

His expression was menacing as he moved closer to her. "There's a small problem with your explanation. I found you by asking around town. I've known for days that you're living here." He took another step forward.

Unlike the frightened, controlled wife she'd become after the wedding, she lifted her chin in defiance. "Then you also learned that my apartment burned down two weeks ago, and I'm waiting for another to become available."

"The perfect opportunity. Do you think that matters?"

She knew it didn't. Not to him. He'd always considered her his property, but she'd never thought he would still feel that way six years after they'd divorced.

"Face it, Lauren. Your knight in shining armor just walked out on you. It's time to accept reality." He looked at his watch. "You and Noah have fifteen minutes to get what's yours, and then you're going with me back to Phoenix."

Libby tried to think of some way she could distract him, but fear kept her nearly paralyzed. Still, she would never let him take Noah. If that meant sacrificing herself, then so be it.

"I have boxes in my car," she admitted. "Where do you want me to put them?"

"All you need is a few clothes," he answered. "I'll get Noah's."

She started for Garrett's office, where Noah slept, but Eric stepped in front of her. "If he knows where his things are, let him get them." He turned to Noah. "Just a few things. We'll get new things when we get home again."

Noah looked to Libby, and she hoped he saw her look directly at the front door and nod. It was a signal they'd used often when he was small, but she didn't know if he remembered it. If she could get him out of the house without Eric noticing, he'd be safe, at least until she could get some help.

"No, I'll get his things," she said. "We'll need that box in the trunk, too," she said as she continued down the hallway. Her heart thudded as she prayed that she appeared calm. Eric would want her scared, but as long as she could keep control of herself, she hoped she could find a way for at least Noah to get free.

Eric stopped Noah, who had started for the front door, but didn't touch him. "Nobody is stepping outside until I say so."

Libby turned around to see Noah shrug and take a step back. She knew it would take distracting Eric before Noah could make a run for it, and as she entered the office, where Noah's things had been kept since the fire, she looked around. The first thing she saw was the phone on Garrett's desk.

Did she dare risk it? Just how brave was she? She knew Eric was much stronger, and fighting him off had never worked before. But if it meant that at least Noah would have the chance to get away, it was worth it.

Keeping an eye toward the hall, she eased

her way to stand between the desk and the doorway. With her back to the desk, she hoped she could remember exactly where the phone was situated. She couldn't turn. She had to have a clear view so she would know when Eric guessed what she was doing.

Taking small steps, she backed up until she bumped into the edge of the large, polished wood desk. With her right hand, she reached behind her, sweeping her arm to the right side of the desk. Time seemed to stand still until she felt the phone and carefully took it from the base. But she barely had time to move when she saw a shadow in the hallway, coming her way.

And then she heard the heavy front door hit the wall and knew Noah was out of the house.

"Come back here, Noah!" Eric shouted, and the shadow retreated.

With his attention turned away from her, Libby dialed 911 and set the phone out of sight on the desk. She was just turning around when she was grabbed.

"As soon as I'm done, no one is going to recognize you."

"Daddy," Sophie cried, "we have to go home."

Gripping the wheel, Garrett shook his head. "You don't understand, honey." He couldn't make sense of anything that had happened, but the one thing he did know was that Libby hadn't been honest with him. She'd taken her son from his father—kidnapped him—and she'd run. He understood how Eric Cabrera felt. He could never forgive her.

"Daddy, *please,*" Sophie cried. "He's going to hurt her."

So focused on his gut-wrenching feelings, he barely heard what she said. "Libby will be fine," he told his daughter. "She and Noah will go home with Noah's daddy."

"Noah doesn't want to go home with his daddy," Sophie said, her words interspersed with sniffing back tears.

Glancing at her, Garrett tried to smile. He wouldn't be surprised if Libby had turned Noah against his dad. It all made sense.

When Sophie let out a blood-curdling scream, his foot hit the brake and he pulled the car to the side of the street. "Don't do that, Sophie," he said, his voice raised, his heart pounding. "We could have been hurt. Don't ever do it again."

Sophie kicked the back of his seat. "Noah's daddy hurt his mommy. That's why they went away. He's a bad man. He was going to hurt Noah."

Garrett shook his head and pulled away from

the curb and back out into the street. But they hadn't gone far when he remembered Libby's scars. She'd said they were from a wreck, but there'd been something about them when he'd first noticed that didn't seem right. Once again, instead of questioning her explanation, he'd accepted it.

"What did Noah's daddy do to Libby?" he asked Sophie, hoping that talking about this wouldn't be something she'd never be able to forget. "Did he tell you?"

"He said his daddy hurt her. He hurted Noah, too. And he had a knife. Noah said he did."

For a brief second, Garrett squeezed his eyes shut. Why hadn't he noticed the signs of a woman who'd been abused? Libby's actions, the things she said, the way she had trouble getting close to people—except for Sophie— were all signs he should have recognized.

Pulling his cell phone from his pocket as he made a U-turn in the middle of the street, he called Morgan's number at the sheriff's office. "Get over to my place," he told the sheriff when he answered.

"Garrett?" Morgan asked.

"Yeah. Just get over there as fast as you can. Libby's in danger." He didn't wait for an answer. As he pressed harder on the accelerator, he glanced in the rearview mirror at Sophie in the backseat.

She was watching him. "Are we going home now, Daddy?"

"You bet we are."

He pulled into the driveway, parking directly behind Cabrera's car to keep him from leaving. He was out of the car in a flash and around to unbuckle Sophie from her car seat. "Damn," he muttered when his fingers fumbled at the button that would release her.

"I'm scared," Sophie said when he finally had her out of the seat.

He was practically running as he carried her up the walk to the porch. "So am I, honey. But we have to be brave for Libby, okay?" When she nodded he held her close. "I'm going to set you down here on the porch," he told her, "and I don't want you to leave. And I don't want you to come into the house."

"Why not?"

He settled her on her feet and lifted her chin with his knuckle. "I don't want you to get hurt, Sophie. Do you understand? I want to make sure Libby and Noah are safe, first."

Her face was solemn as she dipped her chin in a nod.

As he opened the door to the house, he could hear voices. The male voice was raised, but he could barely hear Libby's. What the hell was Cabrera doing to her?

The light in the house was dim when he quietly stepped inside, and it took a moment for his eyes to adjust. When they did, he looked to his left and knew he couldn't waste even a second.

Libby's attention was on the man who had his hands around her neck.

"I told you that one day you'd screw up," Cabrera was saying to her. "I warned you over and over that if you weren't a good wife, I'd kill you. Looks like this is the day."

Garrett was across the room before either of them noticed that he was inside. He grabbed Cabrera by the arm, which he twisted up behind his back, and then pulled him away from Libby.

In a flash, Libby headed for the fireplace and grabbed the biggest poker in the stand.

The man turned his head just as Garrett slammed him into the wall. "That's no way to treat a lady," Garrett growled, turning the man to face him. With one hand, he held the front of Cabrera's shirt, keeping the man from falling. "Libby," he shouted, "take Sophie and

Noah to Paige's house. I'll be there when I'm done with this piece of meat."

With his free hand, he slammed his fist into the man's face. "Killing you right now would be easy," he told Eric Cabrera, who slid slowly to the floor. "It's what you deserve."

"Now, Garrett, you know you can't do that."

Garrett glanced toward the door, where Morgan was walking in. "Yeah," he answered, his voice shaky. "I suppose you're right."

"Roll him over so I can cuff him," Morgan said with a sigh. "We'll have to wake him up to read him his rights."

Cries of "Mom" and "Daddy" filled the room as Sophie ran into the house, followed by Noah.

Libby dropped to her knees, and Noah ran into her open arms. "Did you call the sheriff?" she asked.

"*I* did," Garrett said, holding Sophie in his arms and walking across the room to where Libby was kneeling with her son.

"But—"

"I'm sorry I didn't figure it out, Libby," he said, his voice cracking with shame.

"You weren't supposed to," she said, getting to her feet.

He gazed down at the face that had become almost as familiar as his own. "If it hadn't been for Noah telling Sophie about what happened before you came here…" His gaze moved to her son. "As a rule I wouldn't condone telling family secrets to anyone, but this time it was the right thing to do."

Noah managed a weak smile and nodded.

Changing his focus back to Libby, Garrett continued. "Sophie tried to tell me when we were driving away, but I was too angry to understand what she was saying."

Libby pulled Noah closer to her. "But you did. And I don't know how to thank you. If I'd known this would happen—"

Garrett noticed Deputy Tucker O'Brien hurrying into the house to give Morgan a hand with what was now the prisoner. "We'll talk about it later," he told Libby.

"I'll need to get a statement from you, ma'am," Morgan said from across the room.

Libby nodded. "Of course. And thank you. For everything."

Morgan touched the brim of his hat before he and Tucker pulled a handcuffed Eric Cabrera to his feet. "Happy to be of service, ma'am."

"You can use my office, down the hall, Morgan," Garrett said. "That way she won't have to go in the sheriff's office."

Another patrol car pulled up, and Morgan stepped away from the prisoner. "Stu's here and can help Tucker, so why don't we do that?"

Libby nodded again.

"Garrett," Morgan said, "can you come down to the office? We'll need a statement from you, too."

While Tucker read Cabrera his Miranda rights and escorted him out the door with the other deputy's help, Garrett turned to Libby. "It won't be long. There isn't that much to say. When you're done with Morgan, why don't you take Noah and Sophie to Paige's house? I'll meet you there when I'm done."

Tears glittered in her eyes when she nodded, and Garrett pressed his palm to her cheek, wiping away one lone tear with his thumb. There was so much he wanted to say, but with both Sophie and Noah looking on and everything else that had just happened, this wasn't the time to pledge his undying love. Instead, he simply leaned closer and kissed her other cheek, before releasing her.

"I'll see you at Aunt Paige's," he told Sophie, giving her a quick kiss on the top of the head. "You take good care of Libby, okay?" Sophie nodded. Outside, he could see the sheriff's cruiser pulling away, and he strode to the door, ready to do whatever was necessary to put Eric Cabrera behind bars for a long, long time.

"I'm sorry to bother you," Libby told Garrett's sister, "but I'd really appreciate it if you'd keep an eye on Sophie for me while I take care of some things."

"Mom?" Noah said, looking up. Libby gave her head a slight shake.

Paige's smile widened as she opened the door to let them in. "Of course! I was hoping I might get to see her today. I took the day off. Sort of a mini vacation. Can you stay? Can I get you something to drink?"

Libby shook her head, hoping she didn't appear as nervous as she felt. "Thank you, but no. Maybe later?"

"That would be great," Paige said, while Libby eased back out the door.

"Thanks so much," she called as she hurried Noah to their car.

She'd given her brief statement to Morgan, and he'd released her. And she'd gone to Paige's, as Garrett had asked her. But that's where she changed the plan.

A light mist that had begun when they left the house had started to freeze, and she was very careful when she drove away.

She'd hoped to avoid Main Street, but with the streets icy, she wanted to take the shortest way out of town. She could only hope that no one would notice her, and especially that Garrett wouldn't happen to look out the window of the sheriff's office, just as she was driving by.

"Mom?"

Libby glanced at the rearview mirror to find Noah watching her intently. She knew he was upset and knew what he would say when he learned they were leaving Desperation, but leaving was the only thing she could do.

"What is it, Noah?" she asked, turning her attention back to the road ahead.

"Where are we going?"

Their destination was the one thing Libby hadn't decided. "I'm not sure."

"We're leaving Desperation?"

"Yes."

There was silence from the backseat, until Noah spoke again. "Why? They'll put Dad in jail for hurting you, and we won't have to worry about him coming for us anymore."

But Libby wasn't so sure. She knew Eric would probably spend time in jail, but it wouldn't be long. With one quick call to his lawyer, who would get in touch with a judge they knew, even in Oklahoma, and he'd soon be released on bail. She couldn't risk her life—or Noah's—knowing how angry Eric would be. They were no longer safe in Desperation. He'd find a way to get back and take care of them, the only way he ever took care of them.

She was grateful that Eric was in custody, at least for a little while. It gave them some time to get away. If only she had covered her tracks better, Eric wouldn't have found them. But she'd done all she could, and they'd been safe for eight months. Now they'd be on the run again, and she could only hope she would do a better job this time.

"Mom? Tell me why. Please."

Noah's disappointment and even a touch of panic could be heard in his voice, and she had to swallow the lump in her throat. "I know you'd hoped we could stay in Desperation forever," she began, trying not to let her own emotions creep into her voice, "but we don't have that option anymore."

"But he'll be in—"

She sighed. "Noah, trust me."

"You don't even know where we're going."

Glancing again in the mirror, she saw him slumped in his seat, his arms crossed on his chest. Even in the dim interior, getting darker by the second, she could see his scowl.

"I'm sorry," she said softly, meaning it. She should've done something long ago to end the cycle of abuse. Even before Noah was born, Eric had taken control. She'd foolishly thought a baby would change everything. All it did was make everything worse. And Noah was aware of so much more than she'd ever dreamed possible. For that she was even sorrier.

They drove beyond the outskirts of town and onto the county road, the ice steadily getting worse. Traffic, too, became heavier with people returning home from working in the city. Unaccustomed to driving in freezing weather, her heart began to beat harder and faster. If she lost control of the car on the ice, she was thinking, they could be hurt and so could others. At the first opportunity, she turned off the paved road and onto a sanded one.

She realized immediately that she'd probably made a mistake. The sanded road was much easier and safer, but she wasn't used to driving in the countryside and would soon be lost. Dusk was turning to dark, and visibility was difficult in that time before total darkness. To her relief, she finally saw a drive leading into a field not too far ahead, but as she focused on it, she nearly missed seeing movement much closer on the side of the road.

As the deer jumped out in front of her, she swerved to miss hitting it head-on and discovered she'd overcompensated as she slid into the ditch on their right.

The car moved a little farther before they came to a jarring stop. "Are you all right?" she called to Noah before she could move to look.

"Yeah," he answered, his voice wobbling on the word. "Yeah, I'm okay." He laughed, but it was weak and shaky.

The initial numbness that Libby was feeling began to wear off, and she started to shake. *We're all right,* she kept telling herself, and it took every bit of strength she had to keep from crying. Covering her face with her hands, she shook her head. "I don't even know where we are," she said aloud, without realizing it.

"I do."

Her hands dropped and she turned around as far as her seat belt would allow her to look at her son. "You do?"

"Sure."

She waited, but he said nothing. The ticking sound of ice pellets hitting the windows could be heard in the silence. Her patience was beginning to wear out. "Are you going to tell me where?"

After unhooking his seat belt, he leaned

over the front seat and pointed. "See over there?"

She squinted and thought maybe she saw some change in the landscape beyond a row of trees, then realized there was a slight glow from what might be a yard light. "I think so."

"That's the Rocking O." He sat back in his seat. "It isn't far. We can walk there in no time."

Libby stared out the window. The O'Briens and even the MacGregors were friends of both Garrett and the sheriff. And if that wasn't enough, the deputy was Tanner O'Brien's brother. The first thing they'd want to do would be to call Garrett, and she couldn't let that happen. "I don't know…"

"Somebody there will help us."

If there was anything Libby was sure of, it was that she needed some help in dealing with her past, but she'd never been able to talk about it. Could she now?

It was obviously cold outside, she thought, pushing the idea of getting help aside. She hadn't grabbed her warm coat, and neither had Noah. Just one more expense if they decided to go north. South would obviously be a better choice.

But as she tried to focus on which direction and where they might go as soon as they could find a way to get the car out of the ditch, she knew she didn't have an option about the O'Briens. "All right," she said, buttoning the jacket she was wearing and wishing she had gloves. "Let's get started then."

Opening the door, she felt a gust of cold, raw wind, but she did her best to ignore it. Noah followed and they started the walk toward what she now could see was a long drive, with an arched white sign over it, proclaiming it to be the Rocking O Ranch.

Don't think about it. Just get Noah out of this cold. Then you can worry about what to say—and what not to say.

With one arm around Noah and her hand tucked into his pocket, along with his hand, she huddled deeper into the slight warmth of her coat. So this was Oklahoma in winter.

Lights could suddenly be seen above the row of trees and within seconds a pair of headlights emerged from the drive, headed their way. The pickup stopped and out jumped a man in a heavy coat.

"Nikki said she saw headlights going this way and that," he told them as he hurried them to the warm interior of the truck. "I thought

I'd better come out and see if someone was in trouble. I sure didn't expect it to be you two."

"Thanks, Mac," Noah said from his position in the middle of the seat. "A deer jumped out and my mom swerved a little too much."

Mac nodded. "Easy to do with the roads like this. I'll take a look at your car after I get you up to the house. If we need to get a tractor out, we can. No problem."

"I don't want to put you to any trouble," Libby said quickly.

Chuckling, Mac leaned forward to glance at her, just as he headed down the long drive leading to the Rocking O. "It's nothing. I grew up in Boston. Now that's snow. This stuff," he said, indicating the sleet still falling with a wave of his hand, "is pitiful."

Seconds later, they turned into a well-lit yard, and Mac shut off the engine. Noah scrambled out after Libby and they hurried around the truck to join Mac. "Is Kirby home?" Noah asked.

"He is," Mac answered, leading them under a covered walkway to what appeared to be a fairly new house, "and he'll be glad to see you, I'm sure."

As soon as they stepped inside the house, Libby knew it was Mac and Nikki's home.

Beautiful Native American items were placed here and there, blending with the wide-open architecture.

"Nikki," Mac called, "you were right. There was trouble down the road, but I've brought them home with me."

The dark-haired half Cherokee young woman appeared from around the corner of the entryway. "Oh, my!" she exclaimed when she saw Libby and Noah. "Are you two all right? Are you hurt?"

Mac explained what Noah had told him, with Noah's help, while Libby patiently listened. "We're fine," she eventually told Nikki. "Mac said he'd check on my car later."

"I'm headed back out to do that right now," Mac said, moving toward the door. "You might let Kirby know that Noah is here."

As soon as Mac was gone, Noah turned to Nikki. "My mom was abused by my dad, and now she's afraid they won't be able to keep him in jail."

Struck speechless by her son's boldness, Libby didn't know what to think as her face grew hot with embarrassment and the urge to flee had her ready to run.

Nikki, however, didn't seem to be affected by Noah's announcement as she put her arm around Libby's shoulders. "How awful for you," she said, leading her farther into the house. "We'll do absolutely everything we can to make certain you and Noah are safe and sound in Desperation."

Instead of bolting, Libby burst into tears.

Chapter Eleven

Garrett answered Morgan's question. "I have no doubt that he abused Libby." Narrowing his eyes in warning, he looked at Eric Cabrera.

Libby's ex-husband swaggered, even though he still wore the handcuffs Morgan had put on him earlier. "You don't have proof of anything."

"Yeah?" Garrett asked. "When I walked in, you were not only threatening to kill her, but you had your hands around her throat, choking her."

Cabrera took two steps closer to Garrett. "I wouldn't have thought you were the kind of man who would mess around with another man's woman." His smile was an invitation for Garrett to do something that would get the case thrown out of court.

But Garrett didn't budge, even though he'd had about all he could take, and he knew he should leave the rest that needed to be done to Morgan and Tucker. But that last remark went over the mark of truth and decency. "Legally she's not your woman. She's your ex-wife and you have no claim on her. And if I have a say in it, you won't have any claim on Noah, either."

"I'll be out of here in a matter of hours. And once I am, I'll take care of my family. And I'll make sure you're all stripped of your duties."

Garrett moved in Cabrera's direction, ready to do things he knew he shouldn't, but Morgan stepped between the two men. "We have a special place for guys like you," he told him. With a nod of his head, Tucker walked over and took Cabrera's arm. As he led him to the cell down the hallway, Morgan assured him, "I'll let you know if your attorney returns your call, don't you worry about that."

As soon as Cabrera was out of sight, and the sound of his protests grew quiet, Garrett sank to the nearest chair and put his head in his hands. "I can't believe I didn't see the signs." He looked up at Morgan, who was watching him. "They were all there, Morgan. Every one of them. I worked on a case in Chicago. The husband was a fellow attorney, although thankfully not part of the firm I belonged to. The nicest couple you could meet. And he beat the hell out of her."

Morgan's expression was somber as he nodded. "I've heard stories. I don't understand a man like that. It's beyond comprehension. But I do know it goes on more than we realize." He moved to put a hand on Garrett's shoulder. "Sometimes we're too close to something to see things. Don't beat yourself up over this. You kept it from continuing."

Garrett closed his mind against the image of Libby when he walked in the door of his house and found the man with his hands around her throat. "I almost didn't."

He heard a door close softly and looked up. Tucker had finished settling the prisoner in the cell and pulled an empty chair closer to the sheriff's desk. "If she went to the hospital at any point, there would be records," Tucker said. "With those and maybe X-rays of broken bones there'd be proof. That's all you'd need to toss him in jail for a while. Then add the attempted murder charge and…"

Garrett wasn't convinced a trial would be enough to get Cabrera to do what he wanted. A trial took time, it took evidence, and he wasn't sure if Libby would be willing to go through all of it. But maybe just the threat would be enough to get Cabrera where he wanted him— unable to ever get near Libby and Noah again.

"Let me talk to him for a minute," he announced, standing. When he saw the wariness in Morgan's eyes, he hurried to add, "Don't worry, I know what I can say and do and what I can't. And even though I can admit that it felt good to punch the guy earlier, I'm calm now and will remain that way. Besides, it doesn't look like his lawyer is going to call back real soon."

Morgan glanced at Tucker, who shrugged, then answered Garrett. "Just keep in mind that at this point, you can't make any deals or promises. We have him on attempted murder, so watch what you say."

"I know."

But there was one promise he could make that wouldn't harm the case, and he was going to share it with Eric Cabrera.

Grabbing a small stool, he headed down the short hallway to the lone cell of Desperation's Sheriff's Department. Setting it against the opposite wall, he took a seat. "We need to talk, Cabrera."

Eric Cabrera regarded him with a haughty stare. "So talk, if that's what you want to do."

Garrett leaned forward and clasped his hands between his knees. "You've had your rights read to you, so you know you're being held for attempted murder. There's very little doubt that you or your lawyer will be able to talk your way out of this. Three witnesses saw the same thing."

"Lauren will never say a word."

Garrett wouldn't admit that he wasn't one hundred percent sure that Libby would testify, but he was respected in the area and had friends in the court who would be more apt to believe him than some stranger from Arizona. "You can make this easy on yourself, or you can make it harder. You see, we don't need her testimony. One of the first things we're going to do is get all of Libby's medical records. There's bound to be plenty of evidence against you that this has been going on for some time. We'll also have experts explain how her scars were more than likely obtained." He took a breath and closed his eyes for a short moment, remembering the feel of those scars on her soft skin. "Whether you're found guilty or not will be up to the court, but what I want is signed papers that you relinquish all parental rights to Noah."

"And what if I don't agree to that?"

Garrett had expected him to say it and was ready. "I'll make sure you don't see the outside world until you're too old to raise a hand to anyone." Standing, he picked up the stool. "No matter what you decide, I can promise you that you'll never see Libby or Noah again."

Back in the main office, he replaced the stool and turned to the other two. "I'm going over to my office to draw up some papers for him to sign, relinquishing parental rights." When Morgan raised an eyebrow, Garrett smiled. "Don't worry, he'll make the decision on his own. He knows he's in deep, and this might help him, at least a little. First thing in the morning, I'll bring the papers by. He can talk to his lawyer about it, if he thinks he needs to. But if and when he does sign them, let me know."

With a wave and a promise to return in the morning, he headed home, ready to tell Libby that she was safe, no matter what happened. He hadn't expected the streets to be slick.

They'd been so busy with the prisoner that he'd barely noticed the sound of sleet on the windows of the sheriff's office, and then he'd forgotten. His sister's house wasn't far, but he made the trip slowly. The streets of town were nearly deserted, and just as he pulled into Paige's drive, he thought he glimpsed a snowflake or two in his headlights.

"Daddy!"

He heard the shout the moment he opened the door to his sister's house. Sophie immediately attached herself to his legs, her arms wrapped tightly around his knees. "Hi, sweetheart." He lifted her chin to gaze into her small face. Then he looked around, but saw only Paige. "Where's Libby?" he asked.

Paige appeared puzzled. "Not here. She asked if I'd mind watching Sophie for her while she took care of some things."

"What things?" But a cold chill began to seep into his body and fear took hold of his heart.

"She wasn't specific. Why?"

Garrett sighed and slowly removed Sophie from his lower extremities, then picked her up and carried her to the sofa, where he held her on his lap. "Did Libby say where she was going or what she was going to do while you stayed with Aunt Paige?" he asked his daughter.

"Uh-uh."

He wasn't surprised. Libby was smarter than to say anything in front of Sophie, who was now well-known for repeating what she heard…from anyone to anyone. It was something they needed to work on, but since it had probably saved Libby's life, it wasn't a top priority.

He glanced at Paige, who was frowning.

Fifteen minutes later, with Sophie safely watching television, Garrett told his sister the whole story of what had happened. When she asked about the scars he'd felt and he described them, she nodded her head. "They do sound like cuts. I suppose they could be from glass from a car accident, but I'd have to see them. There's definitely a difference between something like that and deliberate cuts from a knife or other sharp object."

He leaned his head against the wall in the kitchen and sighed. "If I'd known—"

"You can't always know," she told him, pressing her hand to his shoulder. "The closer we are to someone, the harder it sometimes is to see things that might be more obvious to strangers. But you saved her, Garrett. Something tells me she won't stay away long, even if it's only to come back to thank you."

"It's not her thanks that I want," he answered, his heart aching. Somehow he'd find her. If only he had a clue where she and Noah had gone.

Libby sat on the plush sofa in Jules O'Brien's living room, her hands folded in her lap. At one time her home had been as elegant as this one, but she'd paid for that by relinquishing her self-esteem. All she could hope for now was to keep her son and herself safe. She just didn't know how to do that.

When one of the double doors at the entrance of the room opened, she looked up to see Jules enter with a large tray in her hands. "I hope you like hot cocoa," Jules said, closing the door behind her. "Tanner's Aunt Bridey just made a big batch. She said it was to help chase away the cold weather blues."

"Thank you," Libby answered, taking one of the mugs. "Is Noah—"

"He and Wyoming are in the kitchen with Bridey, taste-testing her first batch of pumpkin bread." Jules removed a tented napkin and revealed several slices on a plate. "And here's ours. Noah will be fine. Wyoming has already decided that Noah absolutely must spend the night in his room."

Libby had met Jules and Tanner's three-year-old son when Garrett had brought her to the barbecue. He was adorable and Noah had enjoyed spending time with both Kirby and Wyoming. But she hadn't planned to stay and had only agreed to talk to Jules because Nikki had insisted. "There's no need," she told her hostess. "We'll find a place to stay."

Jules shook her head and smiled. "Try telling Wyoming that. He's decided Noah is now his new best friend. My heart goes out to your son."

Libby couldn't help but laugh. "Noah was the same way at that age. But we really should be on our way."

"I can't let you go back out in this weather. And even if I could, I wouldn't."

Libby ducked her head and nodded. She'd admitted to Nikki that she'd endured abuse during her marriage, and Noah was convinced Jules O'Brien could help. But Libby wasn't sure she could go through sharing her past with anyone, even someone who was trained to help.

"You've been through hell," Jules said, her

voice low and comforting. "Can you tell me a little about it?"

"I—" Libby shook her head. "It's hard. I've locked so much of it away for so long, it hurts too much to try to drag it all out."

"You never told anyone?"

Libby swallowed the shame she was feeling. "I couldn't. Who would I have told?"

"Your parents?"

"My parents wouldn't have believed me."

"Friends?"

"Too many of them were wives of Eric's friends and employees. I wasn't allowed to have friends on my own."

"That's not unusual. It's easier for someone to control a person when there's no one to turn to," Jules explained.

"That's how it started," Libby admitted. "The control. He had his way to get me to bend to his will. I didn't realize what was happening."

Jules leaned back against the sofa, crossing her legs. "Can you tell me about it?"

Haltingly at first, Libby began to describe her relationship with Eric, beginning with how they'd met and progressing to their marriage. "I began to have doubts," she admitted, "and even mentioned it to my mother, but she assured me it was nothing more than pre-wedding nerves. I convinced myself that she was right."

"It's easy to think things will get better," Jules explained. "We all do it in our daily lives. And often it does help. It's better to be an optimist than a pessimist. But in the case of living with an abusive person, it can become dangerous."

Libby nodded, remembering how it had been. "For a long time, I thought there was something wrong with *me*. As time went on, I realized it was wrong, but I didn't know what to do about it. I had no support outside of the marriage and was certain that he would do what he threatened."

"And what was that?" Jules asked.

"That he'd kill me if I left him."

"So you never considered it?"

"Not until the day he hit Noah," Libby admitted. "And then it was as if I finally woke up and saw the reality of my life in that one moment."

"And that's when you left."

Clenching her fingers in her lap, Libby nodded. "I realized that it had come down to keeping Noah safe. I'd given up on myself. A few weeks later, while Eric was away on business,

I moved out. He was served with divorce papers as soon as he returned, and I went to stay with my parents for a week. The funny thing was that after Eric initially got over the shock, he seemed to accept it. He didn't even try to fight the divorce."

"But you stayed in Phoenix, where you'd lived when you were married."

"I had nowhere else to go. Between the child support and alimony, I didn't need to work, but I did find a part-time job at a small boutique. It kept me from climbing the walls. Eric had turned nearly everyone against me, but at least I was free of him. Or so I thought."

Another hour later, Libby explained her reason for fleeing with her son—how Noah had come home with a black eye, and she'd known Eric had hit him. She told Jules about the judge and how she'd lost faith in the law, finally running with Noah to keep him safe.

"We crammed everything we could into the car," Libby said, describing what she called their getaway. "Clothes, mostly, but a few special things we didn't want to leave behind. I had some cash saved up, then we got in the car and I just drove."

"You didn't have a plan as to where you might go?"

Libby nodded, remembering what the underground had done for her. And she'd tried to make it an adventure for Noah. "I had help," she admitted, "but I can't tell you about it. We stayed off the primary highways. When we drove into Desperation, I knew it was home. I'd had enough running and so had Noah. I'd been told where to find a job, and I walked into Lou's, asked to see the owner and then asked him for the job. He hired me on the spot, and I started working the next day. It happened that the apartment was available to rent, and I had just enough to pay the first month and a deposit."

"Do you like living in Desperation?"

Libby felt Jules studying her. "Both of us do. I'd rather stay, but now that Eric has found us..."

"Garrett will do everything within his power to keep you and Noah safe. You know that, don't you?"

It took all Libby's strength to keep her tears at bay. Nodding, she took a shaky breath. "I have no doubt that he will. But that doesn't mean that he'll succeed when all is said and done. He doesn't understand how much influence Eric and his family have with people in Arizona who have the power to get him off."

Jules moved to face Libby. "You need to focus on you and Noah, on healing, not about anything else. What you're not seeing is that your ex-husband still has control over you, and he will continue to have it until you stop letting him. Do you understand that? You're the one who has the power to call the shots now."

Libby thought about it, and realized that Jules knew a lot more about her and how she thought than even she did. "I hadn't considered it that way," she admitted.

"Then it's time you did." Jules leaned forward. "I know someone in Oklahoma City who specializes with these types of cases. Would you be willing to talk to her and maybe let her help you?"

Libby wasn't sure she could trust herself, but if she didn't try... "I suppose it's worth seeing her, if you think so."

"I do."

When Jules stood, Libby's fear returned and she reached for Jules's hand, stopping her. Looking up, she tried to calm her racing heart. "I have one favor to ask."

"What's that?"

"I'd rather Garrett doesn't know where Noah and I are."

Jules nodded slowly. "As long as you agree

to stay here and get some counseling, until you're ready to talk to him I'll make sure your presence here remains a secret."

Knowing she had the chance to see if someone could help her sort out her past and give her some direction for her future, Libby felt better. But she wasn't ready to tell Garrett anything about the abuse in her marriage yet. And she wasn't sure when she would be.

"Any word yet?" Paige asked.

Garrett's hopes vanished again at the sound of his sister's voice on the phone. "No. Nothing. Are you sure she didn't mention something that might be some kind of clue?" he asked again.

"I'm sorry," she answered, "but I've gone over and over those few minutes, hoping there was something, but there wasn't."

Garrett rested his forehead in his palm and squeezed his eyes shut. Everything else was going fine. Eric Cabrera had been before Judge Weller, who denied bail and ruled that the defendant would be transferred to Oklahoma City, where he would await a grand jury decision on whether he would be tried for attempted murder, among other things. Even Cabrera's buddies in Arizona couldn't get him released.

"Why don't you and Sophie have supper at my place tonight?" Paige suggested. "I can fix us something special—"

"Thanks," Garrett replied quickly, "but I promised Sophie we'd watch television together tonight. We always do on Friday, and I don't want anything to change just because Libby isn't here. Besides, you and Tucker need to go out and do something. Both of you work too hard."

Paige laughed. "Don't worry about us. Neither one of us is all that crazy about the social scene, even in Desperation."

"There's one of those in Desperation?" he asked, trying to make a joke. "I'll be by to pick Sophie up later. You enjoy an evening with your fiancé."

Before she could argue, he said goodbye and hung up the phone. With a sigh, he glanced around his office. He hadn't been able to concentrate on anything since Libby had disappeared, except making sure her ex-husband was behind bars where he couldn't hurt her or Noah again. With that done, Garrett had tried to turn his attention to Desperation city business, but he was finding it difficult. He couldn't imagine what it would be like if Libby didn't return soon.

Instead of forcing himself to work, he locked his office and headed for Lou's Place. There was always a small shred of hope that Libby might contact her employer. He knew she was due a check and Lou would mail it to her anywhere, but so far even Lou hadn't heard from her.

The days were getting shorter and the sun had set when Garrett pulled into the parking lot of the tavern. With his head down against a brisk, cold wind, he headed inside, knowing he was a fool to get his hopes up that Libby might be there. And even though he'd told himself that she wouldn't be there, waiting on customers and bringing him a cup of coffee the way she had not so long ago, it was still a shock to walk into the tavern and not see her.

Before he had a chance to sit down at a table, Lou was there. "Still nothing," he said, his mouth turned down in a sad frown.

It hadn't taken long for Garrett to realize that beneath Lou's tough, bald-headed and cold-eyed exterior beat a caring heart. Lou was as worried about Libby as he was, yet neither of them had been able to do anything.

"We'll hear something," Garrett said, easing onto the chair. "Soon." But even he was beginning to give up hope.

Lou nodded, and then cleared his throat. "Can I get you something?"

Garrett hadn't planned to stay more than a minute, but he still felt the chill from the wind. "A cup of coffee would be good," he answered. "Black."

There was a hint of a smile on Lou's face before he turned to walk away. Garrett only waited a few minutes before the tavern owner returned with his coffee. "On the house."

Watching the big man walk away, Garrett smiled, remembering the night Lou had told Libby he would have to let her go if she couldn't work out her child care problems. Garrett still didn't regret that he'd stepped in and suggested that they share child care. And he couldn't believe it had only been less than six weeks ago. How could so much have happened in that short time? How could he have fallen in love, not only with his daughter, but with Libby and Noah, too?

Fifteen minutes later, he stopped at his sister's and picked up Sophie, then headed for home. Neither of them spoke on the short drive, and when they entered the house, Sophie went straight for the phone to see if the message light was blinking. Garrett could tell by her slumped shoulders that no one had called. Libby and Noah still weren't back.

Sitting on the sofa next to his daughter, while she watched her favorite cartoon, Garrett leaned his head back and closed his eyes. Usually she would be giggling at the antics on the screen, but lately her smiles and giggles had become few and far between.

He felt her small hand slip into his, and he tried not to let her see how worried he was. Giving her hand a loving squeeze, he attempted a smile.

Sophie rested her head on his shoulder and sighed. "I don't think we're ever going to see Libby and Noah again, Daddy."

Garrett was afraid she might be right, but his throat had closed, keeping him from answering her. How could he tell her that it was his fault Libby and Noah had gone away? Everything had happened so quickly that he'd never had the chance to talk to Libby and explain how wrong he'd been and how sorry he was for accusing her of being anything like Shana. For a short, crazy time, he'd actually believed she'd hidden herself and Noah to hurt him. He'd been such a fool not to trust her. He couldn't blame her for leaving. He'd let her down, and now there was no way to tell her how much he wanted to make up for the wrong he'd done.

Chapter Twelve

Libby slipped on her jacket and gazed around the O'Brien living room. So much had changed in the past two weeks since she and Noah had been rescued during the storm, but the O'Brien home remained the same calm oasis it had been that night.

Glancing from Nikki to Jules, she sighed but couldn't hide her smile. "I don't know how to thank you."

"For what?" Jules asked, stepping close to give Libby a hug.

Libby squeezed her eyes shut against what promised to be an onslaught of tears if she didn't put a stop to them. "Everything," she answered, her throat clogged with emotion.

When Jules moved away to give Nikki a chance for a hug, Libby counted the many ways in which everyone had helped. "If it hadn't been for Mac, Noah and I might have spent the night in that ditch. And Nikki, you never hesitated to welcome us into your home and insist I talk to Jules."

"I'm so glad we could help," Nikki replied. Stepping back, she released Libby, but held on to her hand. "You're going to the Commune first?"

Libby nodded. "I told Hettie I'd stop there before I did anything else. No matter what happens, Noah and I want to stay in Desperation. It's home to us now."

Jules took Libby's other hand and gave it an encouraging squeeze. "Hettie said she was expecting you. You won't find anyone nicer than Hettie, and there's not a better landlord around than Morgan's uncle."

"Hettie said Ernie is eager to start moving in the furniture," Libby said, laughing. "I can't believe how kind everyone has been. If you hadn't helped us—"

"Don't even think about it," Jules said quickly.

"Now, you have your appointments set up with Lynette, right?"

"Three times a week, for now, but I wouldn't have it any other way." She thought of the work she had done with the counselor Jules had suggested and how far she'd come in only two weeks. Even in such a short time, she'd begun to feel stronger and less afraid. "She's helped me so much already. I can't thank you enough, Jules."

Jules shook her head. "It was nothing. I suspected she'd be a good fit for you, and I'm so glad she is. Don't give up too early, though. Keep seeing her. And even after you finally feel safe again and are no longer seeing her regularly, she'll be there if you should need her."

"I will, I promise," Libby answered.

"Then you're all ready?"

Although getting to know Nikki and Jules had been one of the best experiences she'd had, Libby was ready to get settled at the Commune. "All ready."

After hugs and goodbyes, she found Noah outside with Kirby. After the boys said their goodbyes, Libby and Noah climbed into the car, headed for Desperation. She'd called Lou about her job, hoping he hadn't been furious with her and fired her, but she was surprised to find him eager to have her back. He even agreed that he wouldn't mention her return to anyone, especially Garrett. She still felt uneasy about how Garrett would react when he saw her. It was always possible that he wouldn't want her as a friend…or anything more.

After telling Lynette what had happened the day Eric had shown up at Garrett's house, Lynette assured her that she would help Libby find the courage and the way to explain the abuse she'd endured to Garrett. They'd worked on it for two weeks, but Libby still wasn't sure she was ready. Just thinking about it had her heart pounding.

As they drew nearer to Desperation, she turned her thoughts to their new home, instead of what she'd say to Garrett when she saw him. At the edge of town, she turned to take the back streets, avoiding Main Street.

"I thought we were going to the Commune," Noah said from the backseat.

"We are," she assured him. "This is a short-cut."

"Oh."

She glanced in the rearview mirror. Street-lights lit the car enough that she could see her son looked worried and thought it best to ask. "Is something wrong?"

He shrugged his shoulders and scooted farther down in the seat.

"Something *is* wrong," she said, worried herself now. "Talk to me, Noah."

He was silent for several long seconds, but finally spoke, his voice just above a whisper. "It's the retirement home, Mom," he said, looking out the window next to him. "It's a bunch of old people. They'll treat me like I'm a little kid."

"They will?" she asked, wondering where that had come from.

"Yeah, they always do. You know, pinching your cheek and all that."

"I suppose I should have talked with you about this," Libby said with a sigh. "But there hasn't been time. Hettie Lambert was kind enough to offer us a place there when the duplex burned. There's a waiting list for apartments at the Commune, and I had to make a decision quickly."

"A waiting list for old people."

Usually Noah was good at adapting to changes, and she hadn't worried that he might not want to live at the Commune. This was all coming as a surprise to her. "I don't think it will be at all like you think it will." When he didn't answer, she said the only thing she could say. "If it turns out as bad as you think, then we'll try to find another place." She just couldn't promise it would be in Desperation, although she wasn't ready to tell him that yet.

"Why can't we go back to Garrett's?"

His question caused her to catch her breath. How could she explain to her son about what had happened when Garrett learned she was hiding him from his father? She didn't know if Garrett's feelings about her deception had changed, and she wouldn't risk hurting her son.

"It's better that we have our own place," she finally answered. "And there's always someone around at the Commune, so you won't need a babysitter. Won't that be nice?"

Silence again, until he finally answered, "Sure."

She heard the resignation in his voice and wished there was a way she could reassure him.

When they reached the Commune, she pulled through the circle drive and around to the side, where Hettie had told her she'd be able to keep her car under covered parking. "Let's go see Hettie," she told Noah, as she climbed out of the car.

With a loud sigh, he opened the door and

got out, then walked with her around to the front of the huge old house. Both the house and yard were lit up like a Christmas tree. A long flight of wide, stone steps was framed by two-story columns. A wide balcony ran from the front and both sides to the back of the mansion in true Southern style. Libby imagined the exercise she'd get climbing those stairs and smiled as they mounted the steps and made their way to the big double doors. She raised her hand to grasp the large brass knocker, just as the door opened.

Hettie stood inside the roomy entry hall, smiling. "There you are! Come in, come in. I've been watching and waiting. We're so happy you've decided to become a part of the Commune. Noah, it's good to see you."

"Thank you."

Hettie looked at Libby over Noah's head and smiled, as if she understood exactly what was happening. "Let's go on up to the apartment," she said, moving toward the grand staircase. "You haven't had a chance to look it over, have you, Noah?"

"No, ma'am."

As they reached the top of the stairs, an older gentleman stood a few feet down the hallway. Hettie waved at him, the collection of bracelets she wore jingling at her wrist. "I don't think you've heard, Howard, but Libby and Noah are joining us."

"Oh, I know Noah," Howard said. "He's one of my football players."

Noah, who'd turned the moment the man spoke, was all smiles. "Mr. Williamson! I didn't know you lived here."

"Sure do," Howard replied, winking at Hettie and then smiling at Libby. "Me and the missus moved here a few years ago." For a moment, his smiled vanished, but quickly reappeared. "Hey, maybe you and I can work on some plays to share with the team next practice."

"Yeah! That'd be great." Noah turned around to look at Libby. "If it's okay, I mean."

Libby nodded, unable to hold back her smile. Hettie had tipped her off that Howard was looking forward to having Noah at the Commune. He'd lost his wife less than a year before, eventually turning his loss into a positive by helping with the younger boys' football team. He said it kept him from being lonely.

They told Howard they'd catch him later, and Hettie took them on to their apartment. "It's a little smaller than what you're used to, so I hope you don't feel too crowded."

Libby shook her head as she took in the sunny room. "With just the two of us, it isn't a problem. Everything is perfect."

Hettie patted her arm. "I hope all goes well for both of you. Now, when are you planning to move in?"

"This weekend," Libby answered, and they began discussing the arrangements. When they were done, Hettie walked with them to the main door and reminded Libby to call if she had any questions or needed any help with moving.

Libby assured her she would, and then returned to her car. "So maybe it won't be as bad as you thought it would?" she asked Noah as they pulled away from the Commune.

"It'll be okay. You're going to go back to work, aren't you?"

"Yes, Lou was happy to let me come back," she said. "I'll work the same hours, but I won't have to worry about where you'll stay after school. Hettie said they'd all be happy to keep an eye on you. We'll talk about that later. There'll need to be some rules—"

"What about Garrett? Who's going to baby-sit Sophie?"

Libby bit her lower lip as she glanced in

the rearview mirror. "I'm sure Garrett is handling that."

"But—"

"Noah, I can't answer your questions about Garrett. Only he has the answers." Slowing the car, she couldn't avoid this any longer. She needed to do what she and Lynette had talked about. It was time to face Garrett, tell him the truth about the abuse she'd experienced during her marriage and find out how he felt about it. And about her.

"He's here, Libby." Paige kept her voice low, then turned slightly and looked over her shoulder. "He's been so worried about you. Both of you."

Libby's knees shook with relief, but fear and uncertainty quickly replaced it. This day—this moment—could very well be a major turning point in her life and that of her son. Either Garrett would accept her apology and understand her reason for not telling him the truth, or they'd end their relationship, whatever it was, and go their separate ways. The thought of both options nearly immobilized her.

When she spoke her voice was a whisper. "I'm sorry to have worried everyone. I was…"

"Scared?" Paige finished, putting her arm

around Libby. "I would've been, too. Garrett told me what happened at his house. I only wish things had been different and you hadn't needed to disappear."

Libby nodded and noticed Paige didn't ask where they'd been. It was possible that Jules had told her, but it no longer mattered. What mattered was that she was ready to move on with her life instead of living in fear and running away. But although Paige might accept and understand why she'd left without telling anyone, Garrett might not. That was something she had to face and then live with the outcome.

Garrett's voice could be heard from deep inside the house. "Are you talking to someone, Paige?"

Paige looked at Libby. "Are you ready?"

Gesturing for Noah, who was waiting by the car, to join her, Libby blew out a breath and regarded Paige, who waited for her answer. "As ready as I'll ever be."

But as she stepped farther into Paige's house, Noah following closely behind, she knew deep inside that she wasn't ready and never would be. Not that she could avoid it. Sooner or later, this would have to be done. She could run away and try to forget, but eventually she would end up here. If nothing else, she owed Garrett an explanation.

"Noah," Paige said in a hushed voice, "Sophie is in the kitchen."

Noah nodded and immediately hurried in that direction, while Libby continued into the living room, her legs stiff, as if they knew there was trouble ahead.

"Paige, did you hear—"

Libby slowly turned around to face Garrett, who stood frozen just inside the room. "Hello, Garrett."

With eyes wide, he stared at her. "Libby." He moved as if to take a step, but didn't. "Libby, where…" He shook his head and looked down.

Paige cleared her throat, but neither Libby nor Garrett looked her way. "I think I'll take Sophie and Noah to see Tucker. If that's okay. Libby?"

Libby nodded. "Yes. Yes, that's fine. Noah will enjoy that."

Garrett didn't look up, but gave an affirmative nod.

Within minutes, Paige had both children hustled out of the house, leaving Libby and Garrett alone. Libby was certain her shaking knees would soon give out if she didn't sit down, but she remained standing. When Garrett still didn't speak, she finally gave in. "Is it all right if I sit down?"

He jerked his head up and stared at her again. "Yes! Yes, of course. I'm just… I'm sorry. I never— I didn't expect to see you again."

Not sure what he meant, Libby took a seat on the edge of the sofa, ready to leave, if necessary. Clearing her throat, she began what she'd come to say and hoped for the best. "I'm sorry I ran off," she began. "I was—" She hesitated, unsure of how to explain everything. Should she start from before she first met Eric? From the moment he'd arrived at Garrett's house to take her and Noah back to Arizona? Where? When?

"Libby, I—"

"No, let me talk." She needed to get it all out, every bit of it, then let him make the final decision. "You need to know it all."

"All right."

She couldn't read his face as he stood there, watching her. Guessing it was a part of his life as a lawyer, it still made her even more nervous, and she realized she was twisting her hands in her lap. "Please sit down, Garrett," she said, clasping her hands together. When he settled on a nearby chair, she continued. "Maybe I should have told you about my marriage to Eric, but I could never talk about it. Not to family, not to friends, not even to Noah, except to assure him that everything would be all right. Of course it wasn't. It never was."

"He hurt you."

She was aware that it wasn't a question, but she answered it as if it was. "Yes."

"For how long?"

"Years," she admitted, lowering her head, unable to look at him. It was the shame she now had to deal with the most. It was the shame that had insisted she keep Garrett at a distance.

"Can you tell me about it?"

She shook her head, fear growing inside her until it hurt. When he said nothing, she forced the fear down and tried. "I met Eric when I was in college. I was a music major at the University of Arizona at Tucson and on my way to becoming a part of the Tucson Symphony Orchestra."

"That's impressive." There was a long moment before he spoke again. "What instrument do you play?"

"Piano."

His nod was stiff but polite. "Do you have a music degree?"

"No, I never finished. I quit early in my sophomore year and married Eric." She closed her eyes, wishing it had all been different, but she had to face reality. She'd made a bad, bad choice, but it was behind her. "It was what people call a whirlwind romance. My parents adored him. I was so caught up in everything that I never questioned anything. I was young and thought I was in love," she admitted.

"There were no signs that he was—"

"Abusive? No, although looking back, I can recognize how even then he managed to control me. I was flattered by his attention. I never suspected…" She took a deep breath, knowing she had to continue, but wishing she didn't.

"After we married, we moved to Phoenix, and the control became suffocating. He managed my entire life. Friends, activities, even what I read. We'd been married three months when he hit me the first time."

"And it never stopped?"

"Never."

"What about Noah?" Garrett asked.

"I thought a baby might make things better." Ashamed again, she ducked her head. "I was young and foolish and ready to try anything."

"I can understand that."

Emotion clogged her throat, but she continued. "I didn't have anyone to talk to. I thought it was all my fault, that there was something wrong with me and maybe I deserved it. I wasn't able to be the perfect wife he'd hoped for, no matter how hard I tried."

"Did having Noah make things better?"

"During my pregnancy Eric was careful," she answered, looking up again. "Maybe he was afraid he might do something he wouldn't be able to explain. It was easier for a while, and I began to hope I'd been right, and a baby would change things."

"But it didn't."

She shook her head. "But he left Noah alone. He didn't hurt me in front of him. Not until—" She had to stop again and gather her strength. "Noah was three and tried to stop his dad. Eric grabbed him, his hand raised, and I tried to stop him, tried to reach Noah and shove him out of the way. But I was too slow, and Eric hit him. That was when I knew neither of us would be safe. That's when I filed for divorce and moved out."

"Did he fight the divorce?"

She thought back to that strange time. "No, he didn't, and that surprised me. But I think he was honestly afraid I would tell someone about the abuse."

"But you didn't tell anyone."

"I couldn't," she answered, sighing. "No

one would have believed me. Eric—and his family—are well-respected in Phoenix. I was afraid that even if I tried, something bad would happen, so I kept quiet and hoped Noah would forget."

"So you're telling me that no one knew. Not your friends or your parents. No one."

"Not until now."

"Did you ever go to a hospital with injuries he inflicted?"

Libby studied him. "You're sounding like a lawyer now."

"I *am* a lawyer," he replied, his expression blank. "Did you ever go to a hospital for treatment of injuries he inflicted?"

"A few times, yes."

"Did you tell any of the hospital personnel the truth of how you received those injuries?"

She knew her answer would sound bad, but she wasn't going to lie. "No."

"But there are records, right?"

"I suppose. X-rays were taken a couple of times."

"Do you remember which hospitals you visited?"

"Of course." Something didn't seem right. "Why are you asking all these questions?"

He stood. "I have to make a phone call. Don't leave."

Libby stared as he walked away. Glancing at her watch, she realized it was later than she'd thought. She hadn't expected that telling Garrett would take so long, and she wished they could just end it. She couldn't tell what he was thinking, but she was no longer hopeful. Garrett seemed detached, and he had every right to be. She'd deceived him from the very beginning. She'd deceived everyone in Desperation, and now she wondered if she would still be welcome, once everyone learned she'd lied.

Garrett balanced his cell phone between his shoulder and ear as he jotted notes on a pad of paper. "Yes, there are X-rays. I'll find out at which hospital and let you know."

"Then between witnesses at your house and hospital records, I don't think we'll have a problem with this going to court."

"Good," Garrett said. He'd called his friend and fellow lawyer, Mike Turner, in Oklahoma City the day after Libby had left. "That's all I needed to hear. Thanks for keeping me in the loop."

"Anytime."

He pocketed his phone and the notes he'd

written, then returned to the living room. At first glance, he thought Libby had disappeared again, and his heart hit his throat. He'd gone through his own personal hell since she'd disappeared almost two weeks before and had only managed to stay seemingly calm by calling Mike and staying informed on Eric Cabrera's case.

"There's something else you need to know," he heard Libby say, and he turned around to see her standing by the windows.

"What's that?" he asked, not certain he really wanted to hear.

She didn't turn to look at him when she spoke, just continued to stare out the window. "I don't know how much you know about abusive relationships. I didn't know very much, to be honest. I think I was afraid to know more, because then I would have had to do something, and I didn't think I could. But something I've learned in the past two weeks is that being in the relationship I had with Eric not only left physical scars, it left psychological ones, too." She moved and looked directly at him. "I'm getting counseling to help me with those. I just want you to know that I'm doing something. Maybe someday I'll be okay, because I know

I haven't been what most people would think is normal."

Garrett understood that Libby had a long road ahead of her, and he didn't want to do or say anything that would hamper her journey to what Paige referred to as her wellness. "I'm glad you've found someone to help," he told her sincerely. "I've been worried."

"I'm sorry," she said quickly. "I didn't mean to worry anyone. I was only afraid Eric would come looking for Noah and me. We had to leave."

Garrett moved, slowly at first, and then more quickly, until he stood in front of her at the window. His hands shook a little when he tentatively took hers. "No, I'm the one who's sorry. I didn't even give you a chance. I jumped to the conclusion that you were like Shana. You'd lied, but I was wrong to do that."

She ducked her head again and nodded. "I can understand how it would have looked that way to you. I did lie." She lifted her head and met his gaze. "I didn't believe I had a choice."

He saw the tears in her eyes and pulled her into his arms. "Sophie's missed you and Noah," he said. "She thought you were never going to come back, and I didn't know what to tell her." Libby pulled away enough to look up at him, and he smiled. "I was afraid you weren't coming back, too."

"We're staying," she whispered. "We're renting an apartment at the Commune for now. At least we're staying if the people here don't run us out of town."

He tucked a strand of her hair behind her ear. "There's no danger of that. And there's no danger of Eric ever bothering you and Noah again."

Her eyes were filled with doubt. "How can you be sure?"

"He'll be tried for attempted murder, for one thing," he answered.

"Attempted murder? But—"

"At the moment, he's still in a jail cell in Oklahoma City. Even his hotshot attorney couldn't get bail for him. And he signed the necessary papers relinquishing parental rights. There won't be any chance of what happened with the judge in Phoenix being repeated here. And that's a promise."

Her eyes grew larger and then her smile followed. "I really don't have to worry?"

He shook his head. "You can put it all behind you now."

She pressed her forehead to his chest and

sighed. "I don't know what I can say, except thank you, and that doesn't seem like enough."

He hadn't planned to say anything about her future or his, but he couldn't keep his hopes to himself. Lifting her chin with one finger, he tipped her head so he could look into her eyes. "I've never given much thought to being a father. I guess you know that, considering how I manipulated you into helping me with Sophie."

Laughing, she shook her head. "You didn't manipulate anyone. Unless you're worthy of an award for acting, because I could tell you were paralyzed at the thought of raising a daughter. You needed some help, and I couldn't say no to that."

"I hope that's not the only thing you can't say no to."

"What do you mean?"

He needed to reassure her that he understood she was still on shaky ground about relationships, but he wasn't sure how to do it. All he could do was try. "I understand that the counseling you're working on will take some time. And you may feel scared about, well, getting serious about a relationship—" When she moved as if she was going to stop him, he hurried on. "Just hear me out, Libby," he pleaded. "That's all I'm asking right now."

"All right," she replied, and he felt her body relax.

Convinced she wasn't going to break free and run, he continued. "Besides never giving any thought to being a dad, I also gave no thought to being a husband. I enjoyed my bachelorhood, although I admit that sometimes it's been a bit lonely. At least until I met you."

"Oh, Garrett." She sighed, but said nothing else.

So far, so good. She hadn't outright stopped him, so he would charge forward. "I know this might come as a surprise, but I love you, Libby. I have for a long time, although I don't think I recognized the signs in the beginning."

Her eyes sparkled with what he hoped were tears of joy. "Oh, dear," she said, smiling. "I know I shouldn't, considering the emotional baggage I'm carrying around, but I love you, too."

He didn't think he'd ever heard anything sweeter, and he pulled her even closer. "I want us all to be a family, Libby, all four of us. You, me, Noah and Sophie. You can make that happen if you'll marry me and be my wife."

He waited, afraid she would say she couldn't commit to anything until she'd put the past to rest. He'd understand that if she did.

"I'd love to be a family with you, Garrett," she said, completely taking him by surprise. "But we need to make some plans and lay some ground rules."

"What kind of ground rules?"

"Noah and I are going to live at the Commune for a while, and I'm going back to work at Lou's," she explained. "There'll be enough people at the Commune to keep an eye on him after school, so I won't need child care anymore."

"Oh," Garrett replied, disappointed that things had changed so much. He'd enjoyed his time with Noah. "Okay, if that's what you want. It's just one more reason why we shouldn't put off a wedding, though."

"What about Sophie?"

"She's started pre-kindergarten and enjoys it, so afternoons are the only time I'll need someone to watch her. I've been looking into that."

"Desperation definitely needs a good day care center."

"It sure does," he agreed. "I didn't know there was a problem until you showed me."

"If there was a building or a place big enough…" she said. "And day care providers, of course."

"Of course," he echoed, wondering if she was thinking the same thing that he was thinking. "And if Lou could find a new waitress…"

But they didn't continue the discussion. Instead, they shared the kiss they'd both been aching for and dreamed of the future they would plan together as a family.

"About that day care center…" he began, when they finally came up for air.

Libby laughed and looked at him with eyes full of love. If he never won another case, he wouldn't care. He'd won Libby.

* * * * *

HOMETOWN HEARTS ♥

YES! Please send me **The Hometown Hearts Collection** in Larger Print. This collection begins with 3 FREE books and 2 FREE gifts in the first shipment. Along with my 3 free books, I'll also get the next 4 books from the Hometown Hearts Collection, in LARGER PRINT, which I may either return and owe nothing, or keep for the low price of $4.99 U.S./ $5.89 CDN each plus $2.99 for shipping and handling per shipment*. If I decide to continue, about once a month for 8 months I will get 6 or 7 more books, but will only need to pay for 4. That means 2 or 3 books in every shipment will be FREE! If I decide to keep the entire collection, I'll have paid for only 32 books because 19 books are FREE! I understand that accepting the 3 free books and gifts places me under no obligation to buy anything. I can always return a shipment and cancel at any time. My free books and gifts are mine to keep no matter what I decide.

262 HCN 3432 462 HCN 3432

Name	(PLEASE PRINT)	

Address		Apt. #

City	State/Prov.	Zip/Postal Code

Signature (if under 18, a parent or guardian must sign)

Mail to the **Reader Service:**

IN U.S.A.: P.O. Box 1867, Buffalo, NY. 14240-1867
IN CANADA: P.O. Box 609, Fort Erie, Ontario L2A 5X3

* Terms and prices subject to change without notice. Prices do not include applicable taxes. Sales tax applicable in NY. Canadian residents will be charged applicable taxes. This offer is limited to one order per household. All orders subject to approval. Credit or debit balances in a customer's account(s) may be offset by any other outstanding balance owed by or to the customer. Please allow 4 to 6 weeks for delivery. Offer available while quantities last. Offer not available to Quebec residents.

Get 2 Free Books,
Plus 2 Free Gifts—
just for trying the _Reader Service!_

YES! Please send me 2 FREE Harlequin® Romance LARGER PRINT novels and my 2 FREE gifts (gifts are worth about $10 retail). After receiving them, if I don't wish to receive any more books, I can return the shipping statement marked "cancel." If I don't cancel, I will receive 4 brand-new novels every month and be billed just $5.34 per book in the U.S. or $5.74 per book in Canada. That's a savings of at least 15% off the cover price! It's quite a bargain! Shipping and handling is just 50¢ per book in the U.S. and 75¢ per book in Canada.* I understand that accepting the 2 free books and gifts places me under no obligation to buy anything. I can always return a shipment and cancel at any time. The free books and gifts are mine to keep no matter what I decide.

119/319 HDN GLWP

Name	(PLEASE PRINT)	
Address		Apt. #
City	State/Prov.	Zip/Postal Code

Signature (if under 18, a parent or guardian must sign)

Mail to the **Reader Service:**
IN U.S.A.: P.O. Box 1341, Buffalo, NY 14240-8531
IN CANADA: P.O. Box 603, Fort Erie, Ontario L2A 5X3

Want to try two free books from another line?
Call 1-800-873-8635 or visit www.ReaderService.com.

* Terms and prices subject to change without notice. Prices do not include applicable taxes. Sales tax applicable in N.Y. Canadian residents will be charged applicable taxes. Offer not valid in Quebec. This offer is limited to one order per household. Books received may not be as shown. Not valid for current subscribers to Harlequin Romance Larger-Print books. All orders subject to approval. Credit or debit balances in a customer's account(s) may be offset by any other outstanding balance owed by or to the customer. Please allow 4 to 6 weeks for delivery. Offer available while quantities last.

Your Privacy—The Reader Service is committed to protecting your privacy. Our Privacy Policy is available online at www.ReaderService.com or upon request from the Reader Service.

We make a portion of our mailing list available to reputable third parties that offer products we believe may interest you. If you prefer that we not exchange your name with third parties, or if you wish to clarify or modify your communication preferences, please visit us at www.ReaderService.com/consumerschoice or write to us at Reader Service Preference Service, P.O. Box 9062, Buffalo, NY 14240-9062. Include your complete name and address.

HRLP17R2

Get 2 Free Books,
Plus 2 Free Gifts—
just for trying the Reader Service!

Get 2 Free Books,
Plus 2 Free Gifts—
just for trying the
Reader Service!

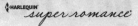

Get 2 Free Books,
Plus 2 Free Gifts—
just for trying the Reader Service!

HARLEQUIN
HEARTWARMING™

YES! Please send me 2 FREE Harlequin® Heartwarming™ Larger-Print novels and my 2 FREE mystery gifts (gifts worth about $10 retail). After receiving them, if I don't wish to receive any more books, I can return the shipping statement marked "cancel." If I don't cancel, I will receive 4 brand-new larger-print novels every month and be billed just $5.49 per book in the U.S. or $6.24 per book in Canada. That's a savings of at least 19% off the cover price. It's quite a bargain! Shipping and handling is just 50¢ per book in the U.S. and 75¢ per book in Canada.* I understand that accepting the 2 free books and gifts places me under no obligation to buy anything. I can always return a shipment and cancel at any time. The free books and gifts are mine to keep no matter what I decide.

161/361 IDN GLWT

Name	(PLEASE PRINT)	
Address		Apt. #
City	State/Prov.	Zip/Postal Code

Signature (if under 18, a parent or guardian must sign)

Mail to the Reader Service:
IN U.S.A.: P.O. Box 1341, Buffalo, NY 14240-8531
IN CANADA: P.O. Box 603, Fort Erie, Ontario L2A 5X3

Want to try two free books from another line?
Call 1-800-873-8635 today or visit www.ReaderService.com.

* Terms and prices subject to change without notice. Prices do not include applicable taxes. Sales tax applicable in N.Y. Canadian residents will be charged applicable taxes. Offer not valid in Quebec. This offer is limited to one order per household. Books received may not be as shown. Not valid for current subscribers to Harlequin Heartwarming Larger-Print books. All orders subject to approval. Credit or debit balances in a customer's account(s) may be offset by any other outstanding balance owed by or to the customer. Please allow 4 to 6 weeks for delivery. Offer available while quantities last.

Your Privacy—The Reader Service is committed to protecting your privacy. Our Privacy Policy is available online at www.ReaderService.com or upon request from the Reader Service.

We make a portion of our mailing list available to reputable third parties that offer products we believe may interest you. If you prefer that we not exchange your name with third parties, or if you wish to clarify or modify your communication preferences, please visit us at www.ReaderService.com/consumerschoice or write to us at Reader Service Preference Service, P.O. Box 9062, Buffalo, NY 14240-9062. Include your complete name and address.

HWI7R

Get 2 Free Books,
Plus 2 Free Gifts -
just for trying the *Reader Service!*

Get 2 Free Books,
Plus 2 Free Gifts—
just for trying the Reader Service!

♦ HARLEQUIN®
Western Romance

READERSERVICE.COM

Manage your account online!

- Review your order history
- Manage your payments
- Update your address

*We've designed the
Reader Service website
just for you.*

Enjoy all the features!

- Discover new series available to you, and read excerpts from any series.
- Respond to mailings and special monthly offers.
- Browse the Bonus Bucks catalog and online-only exculsives.
- Share your feedback.

Visit us at:

ReaderService.com

RS16R